all the best to
Virginia

Susan Barrett

April 17th 88

Stephen and Violet

Also by Susan Barrett:

NOVELS:

Jam Today
Moses
Noah's Ark
Private View
Rubbish
The Beacon

TRAVEL/NATURAL HISTORY:

Travels With a Wildlife Artist – The Living Landscape of Greece

TV PLAY:

The Portrait

FOR CHILDREN:

The Line Sophie Drew
The Square Ben Drew
The Circle Sarah Drew

Stephen and Violet

SUSAN BARRETT

COLLINS
8 Grafton Street, London W1
1988

William Collins Sons & Co. Ltd
London · Glasgow · Sydney · Auckland
Toronto · Johannesburg

BRITISH LIBRARY CATALOGUING IN PUBLICATION DATA

Barrett, Susan, *1938–*
Stephen and Violet.
I. Title
823'914 [F] PR6052.A723
ISBN 0–00–223337–1

First published 1988

Typeset by Wyvern Typesetting Ltd, Bristol
Made and printed in Great Britain
by Robert Hartnoll (1985) Ltd, Bodmin

For Ben

Mort pour la France. Mort pour la France. To live in hearts we leave behind is not to die. Second Lieutenant H.M. Stewart, Royal Air Force, 16th June 1918, aged 20. Tranquil you lie, your memory hallowed in the land you loved. Highland Light Infantry, 3rd April 1918. Sapper T. Minty, Royal Engineers, 14th April 1918. An airman of the 1939–1945 war, Royal Air Force, 4th July 1944, Known unto God.

Violet moved slowly between the rows, ready but unwilling to leave the cemetery. She had found what she had been looking for but she could not stop reading the names. The Frenchmen's names were engraved on black metal plaques attached to crosses made of a pinkish, speckled stone. On each was the message, *Mort pour la France.* The crosses were set in long flower beds where dwarf bush roses grew. There were no weeds. The grass between the rows was neatly mown, and clipped at the edges. It had begun to rain, gently, persistently. Her shoes were wet. She had put on light canvas ones first thing in the morning. It had still been summer. Now, nearing the Channel, it was a grey autumn day. The Tricolour hung dismally from a flagpole in the centre of the cemetery. *Mort pour la France. Mort pour la France. Mort pour la France.* She should not think of wet shoes when faced with so much mortality. There was a stone cross with a metal plate: *Russe inconnu, Mort pour la France.* And then another, just the same.

Among the small pink crosses were white stones, tooth shaped. These bore the names of the British, Australians and New Zealanders, some of whom had been killed in the First World War and some in the Second. *S.C. Holmes, Flight Engineer, Royal Air Force, 9th June 1944, aged 28. Our Syd, some day, some time, our eyes shall see, The face we keep in memory.*

Once Violet had thought this possible. She had been comforted by the notion of a peopled heaven and a man-like God benignly welcoming all the Christians in. Now she thought, like Stephen, that death was the end. The most we can hope for is to be remembered for a while. To live in hearts we leave behind is not to die. *Ici reposent 10 militaires français, Morts pour la France.*

Violet turned away from the large memorial on which this was inscribed and lifted her eyes. Outside the cemetery, the size of a football pitch, lay the suburbs of Beauvais. The roofs of bungalows were visible behind a line of truncated evergreens that looked like yellowy-green stalagmites. She could also see a garden with a group of sunflowers hanging their heads in the rain, and a patch of orange dahlias. A woman was taking in wet washing from a line strung between a pole and an apple tree. Traffic streamed past the wrought iron gates of the cemetery. There was a zebra crossing and, on the far side of the road, a modern church. Just down the road from the crossing and the church, Stephen was waiting in the van.

For the second time that evening Stephen was waiting in the queue for the telephone. Though both windows and the door of the little office were open, there was not a breath of air. The people in the queue drooped against the wall like unwatered plants, occasionally stirring themselves to glare at the present occupant of the booth who was shouting interminably in a language hard to place.

Stephen would have given up the wait long ago. But, for the first time during his six months' stay in Greece, he had been told to ring home at once. His godmother in Athens was the link with his parents who had made this arrangement on his departure. They had said that however happy they were for him to 'spread his wings', an expression which he knew covered their relief at seeing the back of him, they must know at regular intervals where he was. So every few weeks he contacted his godmother, which was easier and cheaper than phoning England. She fed the news back to his parents.

His godmother did not know what had happened; but it was urgent, she impressed on him. As Stephen waited he thought of accidents and illnesses. Would he have to return home at once? This was not what he had planned. He had hoped to stay another month, although the cash he had earned picking oranges was running low. He had been thinking of rejoining Jake, who had come out with him.

Jake had got himself a job in a harbour village to the south of the island. He was washing up. Stephen was not keen on washing up. But he would prefer to wash up than return home just yet.

Meanwhile, some two hundred kilometres to the north, Stephen's Great-aunt Violet lay in a hospital bed with her eyes closed, feigning sleep. It was the only way she could escape the attentions of the women all around her. If she let even a single eyelid flicker open, they were upon her. They had learnt her name at once and this was the one sound she understood in the words that washed over her like the waves of a stormy sea. She could only nod and smile in response. Try as she would, she could not remember the word for thank you. This failure of memory irritated her considerably.

Wherever she had travelled in her long life, Violet had always learnt what she called her survival vocabulary. Even now she could remember the Swahili for please and thank you, good morning, goodnight, how much, how far, I am sorry, I do not understand and I am English; yet it was nearly forty years since she had visited Kenya. It was sixty years since she had been in India and yet, were she to find herself there instead of in this Greek hospital bed, she would be able to carry on a reasonable conversation. Everyone had thought it odd of her to learn Hindustani. There it had not been necessary. Here only the doctor and two of the nurses spoke English, and she hardly ever saw them. It was the other women in the ward who were nursing her and it was to them that constant thank yous were necessary. They were so kind, bringing her food and fruit and flowers, plumping her pillows and smoothing her sheets. It was almost impossible to tell which were the patients and which were the visiting relations. Only a few of the patients never stirred from their beds. Most were up and down like jack-in-the-boxes. Sometimes, Vi noticed, the visitors climbed into bed for a sleep; empty or otherwise, it did not seem to matter. Vi quite expected that one of the many women who came to sit on her bed to talk to her and the neighbouring women would push her aside, pull a pillow into a comfortable position and lie down for a siesta. She wondered how she would cope with this situation. Would she have the strength of mind to object? Would she be able to turf the encroaching woman off even if, as was likely, the intruder had given her food?

Without these gifts, Vi would have had little to eat for five days. The minimum of food was provided by the hospital. It was this dependence on charity, more than the pain in her leg, that made her uneasy. No matter what the doctor said about staying put for at least a fortnight, she would get out and home as soon as she could. Mr Fanshawe, the leader of the bird-watching group, had been keen to put her on an aeroplane. But she had explained about her blood pressure and her doctor's edict that she must not fly. Clearly she could not continue with the party to north-eastern Greece; nor return home with them. There were no spare seats on the coach on which she could rest her leg. Mr Fanshawe had been distracted with worry. He and the party were due to leave Petropolis so she had let him telephone her niece Elizabeth in England.

'Her son is in Greece this summer in one of those Dormobile affairs. He will drive me home,' Vi told Mr Fanshawe with a conviction that was not completely genuine. She did not want to disrupt the bird-watching plans.

Mr Fanshawe talked with Elizabeth. 'I think she understood,' he reported back to Vi. 'She said she will contact her son Stephen, but it sounded as though that might be difficult. It might take several days, she said.'

'I am sorry to be such a nuisance but you must not worry about me. You carry on with the trip.'

'Well, of course there's no question, I'm afraid, of anything else. But I'll telephone to make sure everything is all right.'

He stayed a little longer by her bedside telling her about

the events of the morning. The couple from Wales had left their binoculars in a café; the Yorkshire schoolteacher had lost a shoe in the mud of a reedbed; they had seen three purple heron, a great reed warbler, a moustached warbler and lots of little bittern.

'Little bittern!' echoed Vi. 'How lovely.'

'Very common, of course, but now we go on to the Prespa lakes and that should be really something.'

So now Mr Fanshawe and the bird-watchers were on their way to the Prespa lakes and Vi lay in bed, waiting for Stephen.

Slatted shutters, painted a pale battleship grey many years ago, kept the sun at bay. The subdued light, the stuffy atmosphere, the musky smell – of some herb? – that faintly overlay a mingling of less pleasant odours teased Violet as she lay in bed. There was a familiar sensation about the ward. It was as though she had lain here, not for a mere five days but for a vital part of her life. The familiarity puzzled her and made her toy with the idea of reincarnation. Could she have been a Greek peasant woman in a previous existence? The figure of Nanny Burton came to mind, the black shape upright in a high-backed wooden chair by a fireguard on which a white towel was spread to dry. Violet tried to put some sewing in Nanny Burton's lap. Did those clean, brittle hands hold crochet lace edging? Or a wooden mushroom, pushed inside the heel of a long, black stocking? There was a pair of rimless glasses perched halfway down her thin nose and from them a greenish-gold cord hung looped around her neck. Was her hair, plaited in a bun and skewered to the back of her head, white or black? What did her face look like? Even as Violet strained to recall the features, Nanny Burton faded. But the ward's familiar sensation that had puzzled her over the last few days was satisfactorily explained. This was like convalescing after one of those illnesses, measles or whooping cough, that banished one from the life of the house below and sent one back to early childhood's nursery in the attics to be strictly medicined, washed and ordered about by Nanny Burton, who by then, there being no more babies, was simply kept on to sew and, much later, kept on because she had nowhere else to go; and eventually nursed herself, medicined and washed and ordered about and finally laid to rest in the same graveyard as the other members of the family.

How it all comes back! thought Violet. But of course it doesn't. She could not even remember what Nanny Burton had looked like then. Yet Nanny Burton had been more mother to her than her real mother.

'I would have liked to have children.' Violet's head turned sharply on the pillow, hearing the words clearly. Was this her thought? Had she said it aloud? The women on either side nodded and smiled in her direction and continued talking among themselves. Violet closed her eyes.

The house, built by her great-grandfather on a wooded hill above the town, faced south, its back to the town and the business which had made its building possible. Ten acres of tangled undergrowth and ancient birch and beech had been cleared and other trees planted in much-debated groups. The land had been levelled and terraced; retaining walls, stone steps and meandering gravel paths had imposed a pattern on the clearing; and, by the time that Violet was old enough to run after her older brothers and sister, the land looked as though it had lain in just this arrangement of levels and lawns, trees and shrubberies, ponds and paddocks since time began. It was on Violet's seventh birthday that she received her first inkling of the concept of change.

Half an hour before the gong rang for her birthday lunch, Elsie found her waiting in the schoolroom, staring out of the window at the rain that threatened her mother's tennis party. 'Your Great-aunt Beatrice will see you now, Miss Vi.'

Violet had disliked Elsie ever since she discovered it was Elsie who had told Nanny Burton about the semolina pudding.

'There, so you had forgot. And I don't suppose you've

even been up to comb your hair and wash your hands and it's all of half-past.'

'But I have,' answered Violet, who had not forgotten the invitation to visit Great-aunt Beatrice, something she had dreaded all morning, but who had forgotten to comb her hair and wash her hands. 'I have really.' She stretched out her hands, palms uppermost, for Elsie to inspect. Her hands trembled slightly for it was the first time she had attempted this trick, recently learnt from her brother Tom. He had explained to her that he had not been lying when he'd told Nanny Burton he had brushed his teeth. For he had brushed his teeth, probably a million times. As he was ten, and they had to brush their teeth twice a day and three times on Sundays, Violet thought this might be true. She was enchanted by his cleverness. But now that she was trying a similar cheat of her own she doubted if God would consider it clever. God knew perfectly well that Elsie meant now and not in the past and that Violet knew Elsie meant now and not in the past, and that Violet was therefore lying. 'But I'll go and wash them again if you like,' she added hastily before God struck her down; and instantly repented that lying 'again'.

'No, they'll have to do,' said Elsie, 'for you're not to keep Miss Beatrice waiting, she's rung her bell twice already. I'll take you up, though glory knows I've done those stairs enough times today and Cook's waiting on the best gravy boat, but your Aunt Beatrice likes to be warned about visitors even if she has been expecting you for the last ten minutes.'

Great-aunt Beatrice's tiny head was pushed almost vertical by a pile of bolsters and pillows. Save for two skeletal hands that plucked at the beige-pink quilt, there was hardly a sign that there was more to Beatrice than the little head nodding continuously under a square of lace that covered her few strands of yellowing white hair.

'Miss Vi!' Elsie shouted in the old lady's ear. 'Miss Vi to see you, ma'am. Now what's she done with her blessed trumpet? Dropped it again?'

Violet retrieved the trumpet from under the bed, relieved it had not fallen into the chamber-pot. She tentatively pushed it under the fingers of the hand that lay on her side of the bed.

Elsie had placed two fat cushions on a bedside chair. 'Now don't go tipping forward on that, it's one of those rickety affairs, all the furniture's liable to get broke in this place, you'd think there was no money around to replace with good solid stuff. And come down as soon as you hear the gong or that soufflé you wanted will spoil and I won't hear the end of it from Cook.' Elsie left and Violet was alone with Great-aunt Beatrice.

'Hello, Great-aunt,' she said, and the old lady's head nodded round towards her on its stalk of neck. The hand fumbled for the trumpet and with a little difficulty inserted the tapered end in one ear. The trumpet was made of tortoiseshell. Violet leant forward and placed her face almost inside the flared end of the trumpet. 'Hello, Great-aunt,' she repeated.

Great-aunt Beatrice's mouth worked briefly and a drop of spittle appeared on her lower lip. Then her voice emerged. 'Who is this?' she asked.

'Me,' said Violet, but she realized her mistake. 'I!' she shouted. Was the trumpet the right way round? Should she be shouting into the thin end, while the wide end completely encircled her great-aunt's ear? She could not remember how it had been on her last visit to the bedside.

'Oh yes, Violet – Vi,' said Beatrice. 'My little seven-year-old niece.' With an effort, she managed to push herself further up the pillows and her voice gained in strength. 'Now I want to tell you about being seven. Seven is a very important age.'

A thrill ran through Vi. No one else had told her this today. They had simply wished her a happy birthday. Nothing important was due to happen until teatime when she would be given her presents.

'Seven is a very important age,' Beatrice repeated. 'Do you know why?'

Violet shook her head. Would she be asked to do some great task now that she was seven? Was she now old enough to be told some of the secrets that were whispered beyond her hearing? Would it be explained why Mrs Fraser had fallen in a faint on the croquet lawn, why little pitchers have big ears, and why Mr Fotheringay had had to eat the carpet which was surely very indigestible?

'Because,' said Beatrice, 'seven is a very important number.'

Violet knew she was about to be disappointed. This conversation promised to turn into a lesson on sums.

'There were seven wonders in the ancient world. There were seven pillars of wisdom. There were the seven sages of Ancient Greece. There are seven seas. Which are the seven seas?'

Beatrice cocked her head towards Violet, pointing the trumpet in her direction. Violet's eyes widened in dismay. This was a question she could not answer. She was not even sure whether Beatrice was asking about the letter *c* or oceans. What was she to shout down the trumpet? Was she allowed to say she didn't know? Perhaps, as she was seven, she should know everything.

'Have you not yet been taught geography, child?'

So it was Geography, not Reading, Writing or Arithmetic. Violet faced the trumpet. 'There's the English Sea,' she shouted. 'Oh yes! And the Irish Sea.'

'Oh dear me, oh dear, dear me. The English do not have a sea. We have a Channel which the French called The Sleeve. Do you learn French, child?'

'Tom knows French,' shouted Violet. 'I'll know French when I'm his age.'

'Speak up, dear. Come a little closer.'

Violet got down from her pile of cushions and pushed her chair against the bed. Then she climbed up again and sat with her legs at right-angles to the back of the chair. She hoped this arrangement would not break the chair which Elsie had warned was rickety. She had been quite enjoying her birthday. Now it was perfectly horrid. She listened for the gong.

'There's the Mediterranean Sea, the Black Sea, the South China Sea, the Red Sea, the Sea of Marmara, and – oh dear, I must be getting old.'

Violet leant forward to the trumpet. 'The Irish Sea!'

'And of course the Dead Sea. What did you say, child?'

'The Irish Sea!'

'I suppose that might be counted. How many is that?'

'Seven!'

'There you are, a very important age. Now I'm feeling a trifle weary, you had better run along. You may give me a kiss.'

Was there to be no envelope? Great-aunt Beatrice never gave real presents but at Christmas and birthdays there was always an envelope with money in it. Violet got down from her chair and stood on tiptoe to reach the old lady in the high bed. But Beatrice raised her hand for the kiss. There were rings on three of the fingers and Violet grazed her lips against a square black ring edged with pearls.

'When I was your age,' Beatrice was saying, 'my father, your great-grandfather, planted the copper beech on the south lawn. I shall plant a copper beech for you, child, and when you're my age, you will see it in all its glory and you will remember this day. Many happy returns. Don't forget your envelope. It's on the dressing-table.'

At lunch, Violet gazed out of the tall sashed windows at the copper beech in the distance. It had not always been there. Once that lawn had been a plain expanse of grass. Then a man who was her great-grandfather and Great-aunt Beatrice's father had come along with a spade and a sapling and dug a hole and put the sapling in it and then he had died and Great-aunt Beatrice who had once been seven had grown into the little old lady who had always lain in bed upstairs. All this was an amazing revelation; seven really was an important age.

'Great-aunt Beatrice is going to get up and dig a hole in the lawn and plant a tree for me,' announced Violet when there was a long enough lull in the conversation for her to speak. There was a second's pause and then a burst of laughter from all sides of the table. But Violet was proved right, though of course it was not Beatrice who dug the hole; something she would not have done herself even if she had not been a frail, bedridden old lady.

The envelope, which had to be kept until teatime and opened with the other presents, contained a gold five-pound piece.

The yellow disc of sun had risen above the serrated edge of mountain. The line between shadow and sunlight moved steadily over the olive grove below, stirring insects into life among the trees and dried thistles. The shafts of sunlight reached a blue van parked beneath the olives and for a moment made its dusty windscreen flash signals to the mountainside. Then the sun found, on the ground beside the van, a rectangular blue shape. Soon the valley was under the full heat of the sun and the only shadows remaining were those cast by the interlacing of thin-leaved olive branches.

Stephen stirred in his sleeping-bag, twisting himself onto his back and thrusting out his arms. A trail of ants, momentarily scattered, reformed their line. They struggled up the rounded slope of Stephen's forearm, picking their way delicately up, over and under the fine bleached hairs, and across the smooth skin of his inner elbow which glistened with droplets of sweat. The ants wavered at the brink where a greenish-blue vein throbbed faintly and then chose a path down the arm to the wrist where a silver chain bracelet, hung with a medallion, provided a ladder to the ground.

The ants, in Stephen's dreams, became the fingers of the girl he had sat beside briefly during the night spent at the bikers' festival. He had not known she was with anyone.

She had been sitting on her own not far from the bonfire. A couple of tyres had been thrown onto the fire and the flames were brilliant. He'd sat down beside the girl and commented on the sight: 'Shit!' She didn't say anything herself, just agreed. And then this biker came up. She was his girl. How was Stephen to know? It was not a pleasant moment. It scared him. The biker was from Birmingham. In his dream, the girl ran her fingers up and down his arm, but the biker was there and coming closer. The flames of the bonfire were coming closer too. It was not the girl's fingers on his arm but the tassels of the biker's leather jacket. The biker was leaning on him. Stephen struggled awake, jerking his arm away from danger.

'Shit!' he said at the disappearing dream. His dreams were so real, it was often hard in the morning not to believe they had happened. For a while he was not clear whether he was waking at the festival or somewhere else. Had he fallen asleep in front of the bonfire? Was he too close to it? About to be burnt? With a great effort, he forced his eyes open and, before shutting them again, he remembered where he was: in an olive grove on an island in Greece. He could go back to sleep. He ran a hand up and down the arm that was vaguely tickling, heaved himself into a more comfortable position on his side and prepared to return to sleep.

But the ground now stuck up in the wrong places. There were sharp-edged stones where no stones had been when he had fallen asleep, pleasantly fuddled. He was aware that something disconcerting had happened the day before, something that he would have to think about, make a decision about. Was it to do with Jake? Had he been to see Jake and been offered a job as a waiter? Had he agreed to begin work today perhaps? No, it was something even worse than this. Or perhaps it was just a hangover? Where had he been the night before? What had he been drinking? Retsina, beer, that tsikouthia stuff – pure alcohol? He had been celebrating. Yes, he could see himself buying beer (*beer*! He must have been feeling rich) for the whole table: the Norwegian, the bloke who rented bikes, and the Norwegian's Irish girl, Tracey. 'I've got a job as a driver,' he heard himself saying. Yes, that was it. He had talked with his mother on the phone and he had promised to drive Aunt Violet home.

'Shit!' said Stephen, pushing himself into a sitting position and looking around the olive grove wildly. He ran both hands through his hair, but his fingers stuck in the tangles a few inches from his forehead. This was serious. He would have to ring home today and explain that he could not do it. Aunty Vi. In the van. Across Europe.

He had last seen his great-aunt three years ago. She had come to Sunday lunch. There was nothing really wrong with her, as an old relation. He had several worse. His father's two sisters and their families he could not stand. But he would rather drive any one of them across Europe than have Aunt Violet as his travelling companion. A journey with Aunt Violet would be painfully slow, painfully polite. It would be like that Sunday lunchtime but instead of lasting a few hours, it would be a Sunday lunchtime that lasted days – even weeks. They would keep on having to stop to admire the view, find picnic spots!

'Picnics!' repeated Aunty Vi. 'Picnics were such an occasion when I was your age.' She turned her head in Stephen's direction. Stephen had nearly finished his plate of food; the others had barely begun theirs. 'Do you ever go on picnics these days?'

His mother waited a moment and then answered for him. 'No, the children are too old for that sort of thing. They lead their own lives.' Stephen glanced up as he heard his mother hiss his name at the end of this announcement. She was making urgent, go-slow gestures with her hand.

'What's wrong?' he asked loudly, innocently.

Aunty Vi looked from one to another.

'We used to love picnics,' his mother said quickly, her hand now back on her knife.

Aunty Vi's hand went to the vegetable dish that lay

nearest to her. 'What does he want?' she asked. 'More potatoes?'

'No, no,' said his mother and returned to the subject of picnics. 'Didn't you come with us once to our favourite place, where the two rivers meet? You know, where there are –'

Stephen said he did want more potatoes.

'No, wait,' said his mother.

'I am sorry, Stephen, what was that you said?' Aunty Vi leant towards him.

'Chuck us the spuds.'

'Stephen!'

'He does want more potatoes!' Violet picked up the vegetable dish. 'Oh no, this is the cauliflower.'

'No, he must wait for the rest of us,' said his mother.

'Oh for God's sake,' came his father's voice from the end of the table. 'Give him the spuds and let's get on with it.'

'This is the cauliflower,' said Aunty Vi.

'Don't let Steve hog all the potatoes. I'll want some more,' said his eldest sister Vicky.

'But you said you were on a diet!' His other sister, Claire, lifted the lids of the dishes within reach and, finding the one that contained the remaining roast potatoes, handed it down the table towards Stephen. Aunty Vi, on Claire's right, received it.

'Not on Sundays,' said Vicky. Why she would want to diet was beyond Steve. She was in pretty good shape. It was Claire who should diet.

'Ah, *here* are the potatoes!' cried Aunty Vi.

'Yes and don't you remember,' said his mother in a determined voice, 'the time we went with you, Aunty Vi, there was a thunderstorm and we sheltered in that stone barn and there was a tramp asleep in the corner and we got such an awful fright.'

'No, that wasn't with Aunty Vi,' said Claire. 'That was with Uncle Jack.'

'It wasn't with Uncle Jack,' said Vicky, reaching to take

the potato dish from Violet. 'We were on our own.'

Stephen wrestled the dish from Vicky's hands before she could put it down and began scooping potatoes from it with his fork.

'It doesn't matter who was with us,' said his father.

'Yes, it does if it was Aunty Vi – Steve! There *is* a spoon!' His mother's voice was starting its climb from the measured, conversational tones of Sunday lunchtime towards the shakier, more strident register of housework. Stephen looked up to check her expression and decided to use the spoon. But Vicky had whisked the dish away.

In a sudden rage, he stood up to reach the dish, knocking over his glass of wine as he did so. There was a general outcry, all the usual shrieks coming from the usual quarters. He decided to get the hell out.

Stephen climbed out of the sleeping-bag and staggered to the van, his head lowered because of a sudden, sharp pain between his eyes. It was the sun on his face that did this. He had tried to place his sleeping-bag so that it would be in the shade of the van in the morning, but the sun kept moving, that was the trouble. It was far too hot to sleep in the van. Mosquitoes were a problem too, whether sleeping inside the van or outside. It wouldn't be at all bad to be back in England in some ways. Get his bike together. Go to the boozer. See some mates. Sleep in his own bed. Eat food cooked by his mother: roast pork, shepherd's pie, rhubarb crumble. There'd be bacon, Marmite, peanut butter. And what had he got for breakfast here? Half a fag and the dregs of coffee brewed from the last of the packet yesterday. Not a good situation but one that could be remedied. He could join Jake and perhaps get a job washing up. Or he could go to Petropolis, a town he had visited before, and pick up Aunty Vi. 'She'll be terribly grateful,' he heard his mother say. The implication of an old and grateful great-aunt had not been lost on him.

By the time he had finished his breakfast, he had decided.

Violet, escaping the heat and hubbub of the ward, wandered around the house and garden of her youth.

She started in the morning-room with her hand on the brass latch of the French window. Her mother sat at her desk to the right of the window. It was the desk that now stood in the hall of Violet's home. (She hoped Mrs Blatchett was not being rough with her duster – but she must not be deflected by present-day worries.) She was in the morning-room about to open the window and step out onto the gravel terrace which was being raked by an indistinct gardener. What were the names of the gardeners? There was Sam, or was he called George, who let her help prick seedlings in the greenhouse. (Was Mrs Blatchett watering the tomatoes?) Her mother was planning the menu for the day after next. She always worked two days ahead. 'It gives Cook time to think.'

'Does Cook think?'

That was her father reading the paper in his chair. How strange it was to remember that he had never had to work in his life! 'Does Cook think?' was the sort of dry remark he might make, but his voice? What did he sound like? What did he look like? His face had gone although she could visualize him as an old man, helped by photographs. He had died in 1926, aged sixty-five. Only sixty-five! Yet, at the time, she had thought of him as an old man. And here she was, twenty or so years older than that and on holiday abroad, still active. Well, she added, still active but for this wretched leg. But she would not be side-tracked by her leg, she was opening the window and stepping onto the gravel which gave a familiar crunch under her foot. (Black stockings and laced-up boots? And was she wearing that brown dress she loved so much with a white pinafore?) The sweet scent of honeysuckle mixed with rose greeted her. What a rose that had been! She had tried for years to find the same species. She had planted so many old-fashioned ramblers in vain. She should have taken a cutting before the house was demolished. Oh, too many regrets, too many missed opportunities. But that was the trouble with opportunities; they seldom look like opportunities at the time. It would never have entered her head to take a cutting of the vigorous old rambler that climbed with the honeysuckle to the bedroom windows. Even when the house was requisitioned in 1941 and she'd had to move out, even then she hadn't thought of taking a cutting. After all, she had thought she would be back in the house after the war. The war – no, she was not there, not even in the years of the Great War. She was in the garden before then.

Tom and Richard were home from school. Yes, she would make it the holidays. But what about Betty? She would rather Betty did not join in because she planned to ask Tom and Richard to take her on the pond in the boat. If Betty was with her, the boys would refuse. If Violet was on her own, she could probably persuade them to take her. She knew how to keep quiet and not move around too much. Betty often grew bossy and this infuriated the boys.

So Betty was in the schoolroom, doing French with one of the governesses. Violet could not remember for the moment any of their names and faces and she would not try because she was on her way to the pond. She would not go down the steps that led from the centre of the gravel terrace to the croquet lawn. That was the dull, public way. Instead, she went to the corner of the house and into the tunnel. This was a long, winding, trellis-covered grass path. A series of creepers, which flowered at different times of year, was planted down its length. This gave the tunnel mysterious moods. In late spring it was a cave made golden by the hanging plumes of laburnum which led to a chillier, china-blue passage of wistaria flowers. Later in the year it grew darker, greener, heavier, a place drowsy with bees and the scent of roses. In winter the tunnel lost its secrets. It gave her the same feeling that she had experienced when she had seen the villain who had frightened her out of her wits lying in a box behind the little theatre's curtains, as empty, lifeless and blameless as a glove. In winter she never bothered with the trellis-covered tunnel.

Now it was summer and there was purple clematis among the pink and white clusters of roses, so the rhododendrons would be over. The rhododendrons came after the tunnel and made a dark and threatening place that had to be run through. The earth on the path was dank and slippery. Blackbirds sometimes swooped across the path and under the bushes. It was easy to imagine that the bushes harboured far worse creatures than blackbirds. They probably gave shelter to all the most grotesque characters that you had ever come across in books; *Struwwelpeter*, for instance. Puppets that came to life at night.

She would never have come this way after dark, even if she had been allowed to. The copse, which came after the rhododendrons, was by comparison a safe and pleasant place. The secrets it held were natural. Here bramble thickets and banks of nettles were allowed to grow unchecked, so that her father could watch, catch, and paint the butterflies and birds they attracted. Only a few paths were kept clear by regular slashing, and one of these led down to the pond.

Tom and Richard were on the rickety wooden jetty about to get into the boat which they had made themselves out of planks from a collapsed shed. They all thought of it as a boat, although Violet, eyeing it now from her hospital bed, saw how far it was from being a boat. It was more like an upturned and legless table. Could they really have rowed this thing around the pond without sinking? How was it that their parents allowed it? Did they not know? She could not remember ever seeing her mother straying further from the house than the croquet lawn and tennis court, so perhaps her mother believed it was a sound and proper boat. Her father, on the other hand, must have seen it as he wandered around the copse with his butterfly net, paintbox and easel. But of course his mind would not have been on the safety of his children. Their daily care was not his responsibility. Nanny Burton, Mother, the governess of the time, Cook, Elsie – there were any number of women in the house to look after the needs of his four children. And that was it, of course. Those responsible were in the house. Outside, so long as they remained within the grounds, the children enjoyed a freedom that was in many respects more unfettered than that of children today. Violet recalled the occasion not long before when she had met Elizabeth and family in Kensington Gardens and Stephen had been bundled into a life-jacket to row on the Serpentine! He must have been about six or seven at the time. And there was she, much the same age, about to climb aboard a makeshift table to paddle about on a pond reputed to be fifteen-foot deep.

They, or rather Tom and Richard, had tried to measure it once. She and Betty had been told to sit together at one end and not move. The boys had brought on board a large stone, a bundle of garden twine and a ruler. Richard was telling Tom how to knot the twine around the stone and Tom was doing it his way, which Richard thought was wrong.

Betty said, 'Shouldn't you measure the string first and tie knots every foot or so?'

The boys did not listen to her. They were talking about granny knots and reef knots. When at last the stone was tied to Richard's satisfaction, he ordered Tom to row to the middle of the pond.

'But I thought we were going to take soundings all the way across?' Tom had a soft, diffident voice. Richard's was high pitched. If he had lived, he would probably have barked like Uncle Albert. Tom's voice would have been more like Father's.

'No, that would mean dragging the stone along behind us. It would get stuck in the weeds.'

Violet thought she would not like to be the stone at the bottom of the pond. The water was a murky, green-brown colour and only looked tempting on a sunny day and from a distance.

'You ought to tie knots in the string first,' persisted Betty. 'I really don't see how you are going to do it otherwise.'

'Hard with the port!' ordered Richard. 'Hard with the starboard!'

The table zigzagged across the water.

'At ease!' Richard read both Conrad and Kipling.

'Silly boys,' Betty whispered under Violet's straw hat. 'They are going to get in such a muddle.'

'Lower away!' ordered Richard.

Tom held the stone above the water.

'Don't let it splash, Tom!' cried Betty, holding her skirts tight around her legs.

Tom looked around at the girls and a smile spread across his face.

(For a moment, Violet nearly recaptured the image of his face but, as she looked, it vanished.)

'Oh no, Tom, *please* not,' she said.

Tom was always kind in the end. His hands – square palms, long fingers with squared-off nails, yes, she could remember his hands – held the stone on the surface of the water and slowly released it. The boat rocked as they all leant to watch the stone's sickeningly rapid disappearance into the murk.

'Don't rock the boat, you idiots! Sit back, girls!' Richard had jumped to his feet. 'Where's the blasted twine?'

'Richard!' remonstrated Betty, so teaching Violet that this lovely-sounding word could only be used by boys and, even then, out of adults' hearing.

Tom looked up at him. 'But I thought you were holding it.'

'*You* were holding it!'

'No, I was holding the stone.' Tom's voice was reasonable.

'But I'm the captain. You're the crew. You do it all.' Richard's voice was shrill.

Tom was beginning to laugh. 'It's gone in! It's gone down with the stone.' Richard was furious. He never saw the funny side of things. Tom was her favourite. She had hoped to marry him when she grew up but Betty had shattered this hope, explaining that it was impossible. Violet remembered clearly her feeling of tragedy when she learnt this. She had decided then that if she could not be Tom's wife, then she would never marry.

And she hadn't. But that, of course, had nothing to do with Tom.

There was a long queue at the chain ferry. While Stephen waited in the line of cars, lorries and buses, he contemplated the state of the van with Aunty Vi in mind. There was very little on the front passenger seat as it was a place where the tide of belongings constantly ebbed and flowed through force of circumstance. It was not long since Jake had been the passenger, during which time the tide had been kept at low ebb. During the last few days belongings had flowed back but not to such a depth that they could not easily be swept away. The question was, where to? Would Aunty Vi have luggage? Despite Stephen's desire to be someone who lacked possessions, the back of the van was full. Even without extra things like clothes and food and drink, the space was crammed with fittings designed to save space. Once the property of the Post Office, the van had been converted by an almost competent handyman and driven to Gambia, where it had been bought by an Australian who had driven it back to England and sold it to Stephen one Sunday near Waterloo Station. Both the almost competent handyman and the Australian had been imaginative men, it was clear. The van bore evidence of many excellent ideas about ways of achieving travelling comfort. But sadly the two previous owners had lacked the qualities necessary to carry these ideas to successful conclusions – patience, money and time – though they had both owned the van for long enough. Stephen himself had owned the van for what seemed like a lifetime and he had still not got round to ripping out the traces of the ideas. One particular trace, a laminated panel which the Australian had described as the shower cubicle, seemed to be welded to the roof and floor of the van. Other, more necessary, features, like the kitchen unit, had come to bits the very first time Stephen had attempted to cook a meal. However, Stephen loved his van. It suited him. He had spent the best six months of his life in it.

As he edged forward in the queue, he wondered if perhaps he should do some housework before reaching the hospital. He could smell cheese, which surprised him. He thought he had finished the cheese long ago. There was a polythene bag full of figs and grapes, given to him by a passing shepherd the other day. If they had not gone rotten, he would have had some for breakfast which would have been better than half a fag and the dregs of coffee. He would stop somewhere where there was a litter bin and chuck out some things. Perhaps he should chuck out his socks too. He had stopped wearing socks when the weather became really hot. That was in May. There must be a cache of unwashed socks somewhere in the back. But these measures would hardly create much room. Now he came to think of it, the thing that was taking up most of the space in the back was the bike. This he had picked up on his journey out, a brilliant opportunity, a swap for his stereo (though he did regret the loss of the stereo). It was most of a BMW single. All it needed was front and back tyres, front wheel spindle, front brake shoes, coils, wiring loom, speedo and seat. He had hoped to find these parts somewhere along the way so that he could put the thing together. Now it looked as though he would have to wait till he got back to England. What a machine it would be! He could not throw it out. If he could find a cardboard box, he could bung some of the bits in that. Maybe he could lash the front forks to the roof.

An open lorry, packed with bleating sheep, drew up alongside him. Stephen turned up the volume on his cassette player and let the music drown the irritating thoughts about housework.

Violet lay in bed wondering if Stephen was on his way. She tried to visualize his van and, for some reason, thought again of her seventh birthday present.

She had kept the gold coin in her jewellery box for thirty-eight years. First, it had been too much money (as her mother had explained) for a seven-year-old who only ever wanted to buy a twisted paper cone of sherbet. Later it became far too little money. Aged twenty-five, she had taken it from the jewellery box and for a moment seriously considered using it as her ticket to freedom in London. Although no longer currency, it had acquired a small value as a collector's piece. But such independence would cost far more than the coin was worth. Later still, when her father and then her mother died, the five-pound piece became a souvenir of her happy childhood. She would have kept it as such, along with a box of family letters, faded photographs, Richard's Military Cross, and Great-aunt Beatrice's square black enamel ring set with pearls, had not she been staying with Betty a few days before Elizabeth's seventh birthday.

It was VE day. Vi had ridden over on the bike she called James, a name easily inspired by the numberplate's letters, JMS 26. It was a BSA Bantam and Vi loved it.

'*More* petrol? How do you wangle it?' Betty's loud voice carried from the front door, down the steps which were deep in the fallen blossom of pink may trees, to the gate where Vi was getting James onto his rest with difficulty. The stand often needed a hard kick that could damage shoes, however stout these were. 'I thought you were coming by the three o'clock like last time, in fact we were about to go and meet you!'

Vi always forgot, between visits, how defeated Betty made her feel. At once she was in the wrong: for having petrol, thanks to her war work, while Betty's Ford stood, wheelless, on bricks in the garage; and for coming by bike and not train.

'Didn't I say in my letter? I was certain I did,' said Violet, but without hope.

'Oh never mind, you've got here, that's the main thing. Is that all your luggage? Aren't you staying?' She laughed at her little joke. Of course Vi was staying; she always stayed several days. 'What were the roads like? We'll have a cup of tea and then go straight down the town, we've got our flags and one for you, the children are so excited. The Home Guard are doing a march past at four, and the Mayor and a few other people are going to make speeches. Are you exhausted by the journey? I hope not because we'll want to go down as soon as we've had a cuppa. You see, I thought you were coming by train, in which case we'd have gone on from the station. It would have worked rather well but you're here now so it can't be helped!'

Violet thought of calling attention to Betty's illogicality. It would not have worked at all well for her to arrive at the station and, with the amount of luggage that Betty obviously expected, join the victory celebrations. But it was not the accuracy of words that mattered to her sister so much as the effect the words produced on her audience. Betty thought of it as 'teasing' and expected people to be entertained by her bright flow of chatter. She liked to be amused herself and equally liked to amuse other people. Violet did not attempt to interrupt the flow but simply unstrapped the small leather hold-all that bore her father's initials. She followed Betty up the steps to the house. Her two nieces ran round the corner of the house to greet her.

'Here's Aunty Vi!' shouted Betty, superfluously. 'And look at her luggage! That's all she's brought. I don't think she can be staying.'

Vi leant down to be kissed on either cheek by the little girls. Elizabeth and Diana were dressed alike, and looked alike but for the difference in height due to the two years between them. Elizabeth was nearly seven, Diana just five. Their straight, brown hair was parted at the side, held in place by a kirby grip, and cut squarely in a line drawn from one earlobe to the other. Their mother told them to change out of their grey-flannel shorts and into their dresses. 'Such pretty dresses,' Betty said to Vi, leading her into the house. 'I've just had them made up: green, white and blue flowers with smocking, a pity they're not red, white and blue. We all ought to wear red, white and blue today, don't you think. I'm going to wear my navy-blue suit with a white blouse, I know the suit's seen better days but it is navy-blue which will do and I thought I'd dress it up with a red scarf. What have you got to wear?' Betty looked at Vi's travelling dungarees and leather jacket.

'I've brought a cotton frock,' said Vi, 'but is it going to rain? I've only got this jacket with me.'

'I'll lend you a cardy, now let me put the kettle on, follow me into the kitchen because I want to ask you all the news. What are they saying at the Ministry? Will we have to go on with this beastly rationing now the war's over?'

'But it's not. There are still the Japs –'

'Yes, but that's the other side of the world. Surely our ships are safe now to bring food in. The Japs don't have U-boats round here, do they. People are saying there'll be bananas in the shops soon. Bananas! What does your chap at the Ministry say? He must know.'

'About bananas?'

'No! About everything.'

'If he does know anything, he doesn't tell me. I'm only a driver and a relief one at that. Of course, there are always rumours. They're saying that instead of getting better, things are going to get far worse. The country's bankrupt. The only people that will be all right are the black marketeers.'

'Well, at least we don't have to have the beastly black-out any longer,' said Betty, pouring boiling water into the brown teapot. Vi was always startled by her sister's inconsequentiality, no matter how used to it she was. She followed Betty from the kitchen to the drawing-room where Elizabeth and Diana, now in their new frocks, sat side by side on the sofa with their hands folded in their laps. 'There, don't they look pretty! Jump up and let's see you.'

Elizabeth and Diana stood up and turned slowly round on the spot, their faces pink with pride. The dresses had puffed-sleeves, smocking, and big sashes tied in a bow at the back. But there was something extraordinarily odd, and at the same time familiar, about the pattern of the material: on a blue background there were large splodges of white and green that might possibly be recognized as flowers were it not for the tucks and gathers. Vi leant forward and touched Elizabeth's dress. 'Good heavens!' she exclaimed. 'The morning-room curtains!'

Betty proudly admitted that yes, she had had the dresses made from the curtains that once hung in the old house. 'Don't you remember, after Mother died and you wanted new curtains in the morning-room, you gave the old ones to me? I never got round to altering them to fit our windows. Hasn't the dressmaker done them well? Look at the smocking! And there's still masses of material left.'

At this, Elizabeth gave a wail and ran from the room.

'The poor mite!' said Vi. 'I suppose she hadn't realized she was dressed in an old curtain!'

'And it's got pockets!' said Diana, still happy with her dress.

Vi went to look for Elizabeth who was sobbing on her bed. The poor little nearly-seven-year-old! Vi, prompted by memories evoked by the morning-room curtains, found herself telling Elizabeth about the importance of being seven. And, on her return home, she packed the five-pound piece in tissue paper and posted it to her niece.

*

Violet became aware of a man's voice speaking insistently in her ear. She could not imagine who this might be, for she realized she had been drowsing and was therefore in bed or, at best, having a nap in her chair after lunch. With an effort she opened her eyes and saw a man in a white overall, obviously a doctor, bending over her. Betty knew all about doctors, far more than she did. Betty had been a VAD. Vi had hoped to follow in Betty's footsteps but, just before her eighteenth birthday, the date her father had ordered must be passed before she too could become a nurse, the armistice was declared. 'I hope we may say that thus, this fateful morning, came to an end all wars' – Lloyd George's words to the House of Commons on 11th November, and read later in *The Times* by Vi, had engraved themselves on her memory through the conflicting emotions they inspired. The war had ended and the troops would return; but Richard and Tom would never return. The war had ended but so had her hopes of helping, of action and independence. The war had ended and Tom's friend would return – might return . . .

'Miss Sharpe! Miss Sharpe!'

Whose was this voice? It had a foreign accent.

'It is time you try walking, Miss Sharpe.'

'Walking, oh yes.' She knew exactly where she was and her heart sank. What a pickle she had got herself into! Stephen would never come. It was too much to expect. And, even if he did, she could not possibly sit for days in a rattle-trap of a van. The journey would be too much for her. She must think of another way. She pulled herself into a sitting position.

'I have brought you a walking-stick in order that you try.' The doctor's arrival had turned Violet's bed into the focus of the ward. Patients were calling for his attention; two of the relations were at his side, plucking at his sleeve. He carried on talking to Violet as best he could, with only the occasional placatory aside to the rest of the ward. 'We have problems here, many many problems. This is not England where I have studied. The main hospital is too full. They made this annexe but it is the other side of town. I run between the two . . .'

'You run?' queried Violet. For a moment she took this literally and visualized the doctor jogging briskly through the town, his white coat flapping round his knees. 'Is it very far?'

'Three kilometres and at this time of year the traffic is very bad. I am sometimes sitting in the traffic for too long. It makes me nervous.'

Violet murmured sympathetically.

'Now, how is the leg?' he continued.

She pulled aside the rough cotton sheet and peered with the doctor at her grossly swollen and inflamed right leg. It was not an encouraging sight. On the second day of her holiday she had scratched at what she thought was a mosquito bite on her calf. By the fourth day of the holiday the bite had not disappeared but had grown into a painful, purplish-red lump. Another appeared, this time just above her ankle bone. Both had tiny heads of pus which she squeezed out and then covered with antiseptic cream and sticking plasters. The nice woman from Tunbridge Wells had expressed the opinion that the red bumps were not caused by mosquitoes but by dirty thistles. Violet didn't think thistles could be dirty but the nice woman disagreed. 'What about all the goats? You might have got infected. You ought to see a doctor with those.' Seeing a doctor was not what Violet wanted to do. The tour programme was so intense there was little time spent in towns. She did not want to bother Mr Fanshawe and cause difficulties or delays about a couple of spots which would be gone in a day or two. By the seventh day of the holiday, when the lake of Petropolis was to be visited, the whole of the right side of her leg and ankle was swollen and painful. 'It's like being strangled by a gorse bush,' she told the nice woman from Tunbridge Wells. By this time Violet could barely walk. If she put any weight on her leg, the pain was excruciating. She sat in the coach while the others, strung about with cameras and binoculars, tramped down a track towards a reedbed. The nice woman had a word with Mr Fanshawe, and Mr Fanshawe hurried back to the coach to inspect Violet's leg. 'I don't like the look of this at all. We must get you to a doctor.' The party were peremptorily summoned back from the reedbed, much to Violet's embarrassment, and the coach driven fast towards the town. Signs to a hospital had relieved Mr Fanshawe of the difficulty of finding a doctor in the town. Within a couple of hours, Violet had been examined by the English-speaking doctor, told that she had staphylococci and septicaemia, given an injection of penicillin, transferred by ambulance to the annexe, and put into bed.

'Ah,' said the doctor, now prodding at the edge of the swollen area. Violet flinched. 'Ah, it still hurts, of course. But it is much much better. No problem. Let's see if we can put our weight on it.'

My weight is quite enough on its own, thought Violet, moving her leg gingerly to the side of the bed. 'I've become a little stiff, lying in bed like this.' She stood, gasped as the change of position sent shooting pains through her leg, and sat down. 'Oh dear,' she said. 'Just a moment,' she told the doctor. 'Can you see my slippers? And dressing-gown,' she added. While he asked the women around him to find these, she gathered her courage. She was determined to walk. The doctor was right; she had lain in bed long enough.

'I ask you to walk,' said the doctor handing her the dressing-gown, 'because we have a telephone call from Mrs Winfield in England. She says that she has contacted her son and that he will come for you. Now my professional opinion is what I said to you first of all. You should not travel for at least another week. You should stay in bed with your leg up. There are your slippers. You only need the left one. The right one will not fit on yet.'

I only need the left one! And Violet held two galoshes in her hand. For a second, as she pushed her left foot into the slipper, Violet felt again the sickening rush of fresh horror, and embarrassment at her mistake.

'How foolish of me,' she said to the doctor. 'But another week! I am certainly not going to stay here that long.' With the help of the doctor's arm, she managed to stand. 'I'll be up and about in no time.'

'Yes, that is right. My professional opinion is overthrown by necessity. We have many problems in the hospital. We do not have enough beds and nurses. As you have the means to leave, it is best you go.'

'But when is Patrick coming?' The prospect of sudden departure filled Violet with dismay. Her leg was throbbing unmercifully. She longed to be back in bed, dreaming of the past.

'Your nephew? Is he not called Stephen? Today, I presume. You must be ready. Now try the walking. Take the stick. I will hold the other arm. There, how is it?'

Stephen . . . and she had called him Patrick. She must concentrate on the present. Leaning heavily on the stick and the doctor's arm, she swung both feet forward, brushing the toes of her right foot along the dusty mosaic floor. 'I think I'll need a sock,' she said.

'Bravo! Bravo!' The women applauded her progress.

'Your nephew will have a sock,' said the doctor, glancing at his watch. He suddenly broke into a stream of loud Greek, abandoning her arm as he did so and rushing from the ward. The stick slid from Violet's hand and her weight was thrown onto her right foot. She tottered but at once there was a woman supporting her on either side. They helped her limp up and down the corridor outside the ward and were reluctant to let her replace their arms with the stick. Very soon she felt she had tried walking for long enough and steered her party of supporters back to the ward. There she found her bed had been stripped and remade and a woman with her leg in plaster was being levered into it.

Once across the chain ferry, Stephen felt he had begun his journey back to England although he had yet to go to Petropolis to collect his aunt. He began to think of his family, last seen in early April. He thought of them fondly, the intervening months having washed away the memory of the friction and quarrels that had led to his departure for Greece. He imagined his arrival home: he would hoot the horn loudly as he turned in at the gate. The dog would bark, the front door would open and, led by the dog, Vicky and Claire and his mother and father would rush out, waving, smiling, shouting . . . it would be a great welcome. His family were good at welcomes. Even the regular arrival of the postman caused a stir.

Stephen smiled as he turned north towards the Preveza ferry – but then remembered: Vicky and Claire had left home. How odd of him to be visualizing his home as it was a few years ago. It was as though he imagined his six-months' absence as a kind of Rip Van Winkle sleep, one that returned him to an earlier time. Vicky and Claire now shared a house with three others in Ealing and both worked in television studios, doing jobs that had grand but unrevealing titles. They came home for the occasional weekend but there was no reason to suppose that they would be at home, even if it was a weekend when he got back. The dog had died too. His mother had told him this in a letter. But until he witnessed for himself the absence of the dog, he could not believe in its death. He tried to rearrange the picture in his mind. He would turn in at the gate, hooting his horn, the front door would open and his mother and father – but no, his father was bound to be out.

So, there was his mother to welcome him. His mother he looked forward to seeing. She was a very certain object in his life, someone who would always be there to welcome him; someone who would always be on his side no matter what happened. His father would surely support him equally but Stephen did not have the same implicit faith that this would be the case. He knew his father loved him; but his father's love did not give him the same confidence as did his mother's love. It was an anxious love that expected more from Stephen and, as a consequence, made him less sure of that love, his father and himself.

Stephen's father was a doctor. This meant that he devoted his good temper, and ability to listen, to his patients. He was well aware that by the time he got home, his reserves were well-nigh exhausted; so he would make a conscious effort to be as calm and as encouraging to his family as he was to his patients. Stephen found these efforts far more irritating than the short temper which sometimes burst through the fabric. The short temper was, after all, natural; the doctor–patient relationship was not. Of all the members of the family, Stephen was the one most often treated like a patient – except on the rare occasions he was ill, when he would be told he was perfectly fit and healthy. He could almost see the case history being written, and not simply its present and past: he suspected that his father had already written its future.

He had a good idea how such a history would read. Stephen Anthony Winfield, born 1967. Usual childhood innoculations. Stomach pains (psychosomatic). Hay fever (psychosomatic). Cut forehead. That could not have been psychosomatic. Stitches had been required. He'd fallen off the garage roof. It was the first of a number of visits to the emergency department of the local hospital. His father was never at home when the accidents happened. 'Accident-prone', would definitely have been written in the case history. Stephen had always been falling off things. He had scars all over his body that, like photographs in an album, evoked events.

How would the case history continue? Age 6 to 10 – well, his father would probably have been pleased with him then. Shows promise, he would have written. Stephen had had good marks at his primary school. He had taken part in school plays and in sports. He had won the hop, skip and jump. In his last year he had even received the form prize. 11 to 14 – uncertain progress, trouble beginning. Although Stephen was convinced he had only borrowed the school hamster, and had only put it in the refrigerator to cool down after it had overheated in his bath, the school and his parents had taken a different view. They had called it theft, and cruelty to animals. The aspect of genuine scientific research and thirst for knowledge – could hamsters swim? – had eluded their attention. 'Criminal tendencies', Stephen imagined his father writing at this point.

Age 14 to 16, and now pages would have been written. Insubordination, reluctance to accept authority. Broken toe through kicking maths teacher. Unnatural weight gain. Diet: wholemeal bread, fruit and veg, no fried food, no crisps, no chocolate. The diet was given up after less than a week. Stephen had exerted pressure on his mother, who loved fried food, crisps and chocolate. Age 15: Runs away from home. Consternation among family members. Stephen eventually rings from distant pub. Cause of trouble? He could no longer remember exactly what had happened except that it had something to do with school. No matter – whatever his father had written in this mythical case history would be quite a different story.

Age 16½: Acne. Leaves school, having failed two out of three O-levels. But he had got three CSEs! Why had his parents been so disappointed? He thought he had done amazingly well, considering he had not bothered with the exams at all. His parents had never grasped the fact that CSE at grade 1 was considered the equivalent of an O-level. He had got two grade 2s, which was after all only one down from a grade 1. 'Crisis', his father might have written at this point. *He* had seemed to suffer a crisis, certainly. Stephen for his part had been having a good time. He had left school. It was summer. He'd had great times on his bike with mates, scrambling on the downs at night, roaring down to the sea and back. The only frustration had been his age. He had been still confined to a 50 cc. That was the cause of one of the visits of the police to his home. It had been sheer bad luck that there'd been a pig car around just as he'd been having a bit of a burn on a mate's 500. Who would expect the police to be parked in that particular lay-by at that particular time of night, and who would expect anyone in a Capri to cross a minor road so slowly? He'd told the copper that they ought to ban anyone over fifty from driving. If the old bag had been going at a decent speed, she would have been across before he turned the corner. The whole world was against bikers, that was the trouble. Nobody had praised his skill in avoiding the Capri. It was he who had gone into the hedge, not her, and it was her fault. The memory of this still wound him up, and, as he joined the queue for the ferry to Preveza, he vented his anger aloud.

A man clambering down from the lorry in front paused, his attention attracted by Stephen's loud exclamations and the way he was banging his hands on the steering wheel. The man reached the ground and, with a swagger of his hips, moved slowly towards Stephen's side window, placing his hand on the van's bonnet as he did so. Stephen rapidly assimilated several facts. The man was a gypsy. He was well built. He had misinterpreted Stephen's gestures. Stephen put out a hand to wind up the window but already the man's head was there, very close. Stephen went through a variety of placatory expressions and signs and after a few long seconds the man moved away.

Stephen had intended to stretch his legs. There was a stall selling ice-cream and soft drinks. But he decided not to get out in case the gypsy misinterpreted this too. He saw now that the place was swarming with gypsies. The lorry in front was piled high with blankets, brightly coloured bundles, upturned chairs and, packed in one corner, four miserable sheep. Two women were chasing a hen among the eucalyptus trees, to the side of the road. They were barefoot and as they bent low, their full, pleated skirts brushed the ground as they tried to drive the hen into a bush where they might catch it. With the agility of a tackled football forward, the hen bypassed the women's outstretched hands and fled away squawking. The women straightened and turned to each other, laughing and commenting in loud voices. They gave up the chase. Perhaps it had not been their hen at all. They turned and noticed Stephen's gaze. He looked away fast and bent to search for a map which not so long ago he had seen on the floor beneath the passenger seat. He heard a scratching and tapping sound on his side of the van. To his relief, he found the map and sat back to open it up and hide behind it. Out of the corner of his eye, he saw that there was no one at the window. The two hen-chasers had not approached. But the scratching and tapping continued. Could it be the hen? Was the hen knocking on the door, seeking sanctuary from the gypsies? Cautiously, so as not to attract the attention of anyone watching his movements, he leant out of the window. Directly below was a small boy of about four or five, gazing up at him while his little hands scrabbled at the car door. On seeing Stephen, the boy immediately raised a hand, palm outstretched, and began chanting in a small, whining voice. He had a shock of coarse fair hair and a round brown face smeared with pink ice-cream. But it was his eyes that held Stephen's attention. They stared, perfectly open, round and brown, straight into Stephen's. The gaze was blank and seemed quite unconnected with the repetitive chant issuing from the boy's mouth. The eyes looked, while the mouth begged. Stephen smiled, wanting to prompt a response in the boy's eyes. But the boy stared on, while the chant grew louder and more insistent. A coin placed in the little outstretched palm was all that was required as far as the boy was concerned. Stephen could spare a few drachmas now that he was going to meet Aunty Vi. But if he gave something to the little boy, what then? He knew that as soon as the palm felt the money, the fingers would curl around the coin and the boy would be off without a smile. All the other gypsies roaming up and down the line of waiting cars would be at the van door. Stephen did not want this. What he wanted was to remove the blankness from the boy's gaze.

A year ago he had spent a night at a folk festival. He had got talking with some guys who said they were camping nearby. Their way of life sounded attractive: living in a bus, staying a while in one place, moving on to the next. He liked their outlook. He liked the way they talked and the things they said. He bought some beer and went with them to see their set-up. He said he'd get hold of a van and join them.

He could no longer take the boy's stare. He wound up the window.

Age 17, he continued in his father's handwriting. Crisis after crisis. His parents had come up with a series of impossible ideas. His father had even suggested the merchant navy, and his mother had returned one day with the Sunday joint and talked of trainee butchers. Meanwhile, Stephen drew supplementary benefit, slept in the daytime, rode (or mended) his bike at night, passed his bike- and car-driving tests, and, the summer evening following the folk festival, decided what he wanted to do.

'Join the Peace Convoy!' Had his mother been an opera singer, her voice would have shattered all the glasses that she was drying after their dinner party.

'What's the Peace Convoy?' asked Stephen. 'That's not what I said.'

'It sounds just like them. A load of hippies living in all kinds of clapped-out cars and buses and things. There are awful stories about them, drugs, children running wild, stealing, they've no respect for property or the law, I absolutely forbid you, Stephen, to join them.' She could hardly get the words out from fright.

'Mother, I only said I wanted to team up with some mates and live in a van. You and Dad keep saying I ought to do something. Well, now I'm going to. You should be glad. You won't have to put up with me any longer.' He should have known that this sort of remark, intended to soften them up, unleashed a whole spiel about loving him and not wanting him to leave home, just wanting the best for him, and being anxious to help him and so on and so forth. But the outcome was satisfactory. By the time his parents had cleared the kitchen and were ready for bed, they had almost promised that he would get the money for a van on his eighteenth birthday on one condition: that he did not join the Peace Convoy.

The next day he went to find his mates in their bus to discover if they were called the Peace Convoy. But things took an unpleasant turn. The bus was nowhere to be seen. He was simply asking around to discover if anyone knew where it and his mates might be. He was dressed normally in his jeans and T-shirt, his hair was uncombed, his doss-rag unwashed; he didn't consider he looked any different from all the others wandering among the tents and vans and buses and camp fires and tethered goats and grubby children. But for some reason (could it be the crash helmet and leather jacket he was carrying?) five or six people came up and told him to clear off. They told him what they would do if he didn't leave at once. It was possible they had mistaken him for someone else, but they weren't the kind to argue with. As he left, he saw the people in a new light. They looked hostile. Even the children were jeering at him. He was shocked at the words the little four- and five-year-olds knew and the way they yelled them.

This experience had been a deep disappointment to him. The evening before, he had felt that at last he had found a way of life, and people, that would suit him. That hope had been short-lived and once again his life had become as pointless as it had ever been, and as it ever promised to be.

The little gypsy boy was still staring up at him. Stephen was conscious of the stare although his own eyes were on the map.

Cars were now driving past on the opposite side of the road. A ferry had docked. Slowly the queue began to move. The scratching and tapping continued with renewed vigour on the van door. Stephen laid aside the map and started the engine. He engaged gear and began to edge forward. Almost without thinking, his hand went into his back pocket and found a fifty-drachma note. He unwound the window and let the paper money flutter to the ground. A few yards further on, he glanced in the wing mirror and caught a glimpse of the little boy. He was holding the money in his hand and staring at Stephen's reflection in the wing mirror. Stephen smiled and waved but when he turned to look out of the window, the little boy had gone.

Violet had first of all been glad to find herself up and dressed. Sitting on a bench in the hospital waiting-room, she had watched the comings and goings with interest. But now she was beginning to worry. Her watch, which every so often she consulted, showed it was four o'clock.

She had been under the impression, when the doctor had helped her out of bed, that this was just the first of a series of short exercise periods. But then the doctor had disappeared. So too, in a manner of speaking, had her bed. Another woman lay on it. Vi had been ushered to a bathroom by a nurse who handed her the clothes she had been wearing on admittance. Once dressed, she was led to the waiting-room and left. She had sat there quite happily until a porter had brought her suitcase, her straw hat, her umbrella and her handbag and stacked them in a corner by the bench. This was alarming. Had the hospital really finished with her? Was it definite that Stephen would collect her today? What exactly had the doctor said? She did not feel at all ready to leave the hospital, nor was she certain that Stephen really was on his way. What would become of her if he did not turn up tonight? Would she be able to order a taxi and get herself to a hotel? The precariousness of her situation struck her forcibly.

Perhaps Edith Jenkins, her neighbour, was right. She should not, at her age, go off on foreign holidays on her own. 'But it's not on my own at all. It's with a group, all arranged.' 'And if something goes wrong? If you get ill, for instance?' Edith was a year older than Violet and still got down on her hands and knees to weed her rose bed. 'Isn't she a wonder?' Mrs Blatchett often remarked. Violet thought that Edith only did it to show off. She could easily use a hoe. Whenever Violet had a visitor, Edith would always be in her front garden doing something marvellous for her age. But she never went on holiday. She said she didn't need holidays, her whole life was a holiday, a working one, mind you. Edith even offered to clip Violet's box hedge. She offered every year and Violet always replied that the Boy Scouts would do it in the autumn bob-a-job week. She liked to let it flower. Edith dead-headed her roses well before the roses had died. She spring-cleaned in January; ordered her winter coke in the spring; bought her Christmas presents in June; and spent the autumn planting spring bulbs, indoors as well as out. Her house at Christmas time was heady with the scent of hyacinths.

But Edith never stirred from her house, and here was Violet, marooned with crippling carbuncles in a country where she could not speak the language. Every so often, as she sat on the bench, someone would come up and say something and she could only smile foolishly until they moved away. Now an old man in a shiny grey suit and white collarless shirt came and sat beside her. He had a walking-stick which he held between his spread knees, and he rested his hands on its curved handle.

'You American?' he asked brusquely. The words emerged

from beneath a drooping yellow thatch of moustache.

Violet began to reply but found she had to clear her throat. She had hardly spoken for days. 'No, English. From England.' She rearranged her crumpled dress.

'Ah. Ah.' The old man tapped his stick on the ground, as though in approval. 'Ah,' he said again, and then went on, 'American.' He lifted a hand from the stick to slap his chest. 'Chicago.'

'Oh really?' Violet turned with interest. 'You're from Chicago?'

'Yep. Chicago.'

Violet prepared herself for conversation. This would take her mind off her worries. 'I've visited the States, but I'm afraid I have never been to Chicago. Its position must be wonderful, on the lake . . .' She let the words trail for him, but there was no response. 'Very big, of course,' she went on. 'It is a very large place.' This time she would give him longer to reply. Perhaps he did not want a conversation at all.

After a while he spoke. 'Yep. Chicago,' he said. 'Good place, good people.'

'That's nice,' said Violet. The conversation might not have the sparkling quality she would have enjoyed but at least it was an exchange of words. She had realized he was a Greek–American. 'And how long have you lived there?'

'Dirdy,' he said. 'Yep, dirdy.'

'Dirty?' she queried, flummoxed for a moment.

'Dirdy year.'

'Oh yes, I see. So you must have gone out there in, let me see, the 1950s?'

'Nah, nah, nah.' He shook his head and thumped his stick, rather angrily it seemed, on the floor. 'The year dirdy. Ninedeen dirdy.'

'You went out in 1930? So you've lived there fifty, very nearly sixty years! Gracious me!' She wondered that he had not learnt more English, but she knew that foreign communities kept themselves very much to themselves. It was like the English in India. When she visited Betty in India, she had been surprised at how separate the life was. But that had been naive of her. They had laughed at her ideas, her lack of understanding.

The old man had said something. 'I'm sorry, I didn't quite catch that?'

'The war, the war. Ninedeen dirdy Chicago. The war, Greece. Fight here. Bad times. Albania.' He raised his stick, pointed it at a family crossing the room and made gun noises. 'And cold! By God, cold!' After the slow start, he was getting into the swing. A few people had edged nearer to listen in admiration. They began to ask him questions. Violet understood the questions concerned her, for the old man broke off to point to her swollen leg with his stick and ask, 'What's the problem?'

Her description of the mosquito bites that had become carbuncles led to a description of the bird-watching trip. It was surprising how much information could be exchanged with the help of theatrical gestures and the old man's half-remembered English. He was called Tony and was the father of the woman now sitting on Violet's right. She was called Aspasia. Aspasia had come to the hospital with her husband and two neighbours to visit her daughter, who had given birth to a son two days before. They were now waiting for mother and baby to wake from an afternoon sleep. 'My goodness!' exclaimed Violet. 'That makes you a great-grandfather!' In turn, they learnt that Violet had no husband and lived on her own, which they seemed to find upsetting. But they perked up when she told them about her two nieces and their families. She found the photographs she always carried in her handbag and passed them around. There was the one of Diana and her family sitting on a Cornish beach, which elicited comments on the number of clothes they were all wearing and how very far north England lay. And there was one of Elizabeth and her family, taken a few years ago when she'd been invited over to Sunday lunch. Violet pointed out her great-nephew Stephen and explained that it was Stephen who would be collecting her from the hospital. 'Good,' they all said in English. 'Good, good.' But whether this referred to Stephen's looks or the fact that a member of her family would be with her soon was unclear.

When the photograph was returned to her, she looked closely at Stephen. That occasion had been the last time she had seen him. He must have been fifteen or perhaps sixteen then. It had been a little difficult persuading the family to sit together so that she could take the photograph. Vicky and Claire wanted to go and check in a mirror that their hair was all right; Elizabeth was worrying that the cauliflower would overcook; and Stephen did not want to be photographed at all. The photograph showed this reluctance. He stood apart from the others who had arranged themselves nicely on the patio. Elizabeth, Vicky and Claire sat, with smiles on their faces, at the round white table, the striped umbrella at a jaunty angle above them. David stood at the open French window, holding up a bottle of gin for the camera's benefit. But Stephen stood on the wrong side of the umbrella and scowled at his feet. No, thought Violet, they cannot be saying 'good' to his looks. His hair hung straight down over his forehead and ears, rather like a cloche hat. His nose looked out of proportion to his face. His shirt was not fully tucked into his trousers.

'Big,' said Tony. 'A big boy.'

Certainly, three years ago he had been as tall as Elizabeth. His head was level with the top of the umbrella. But he would be taller now. 'Yes,' said Violet with a sigh. She did not think that Stephen, tall or not, would be coming to get her. Her watch said five-fifteen.

By midday Stephen was parked in a side-street near the main square of Petropolis. His mother had not given him the name or address of the hospital and he presumed that there would be only one in the town. He planned to ask for directions in a shop. He was hungry but had decided not to eat until he had picked up Aunty Vi. She would be paying for lunch and for all his expenses from now on. For the same reason he had not filled the van with petrol.

A shepherd's cloak, hanging above a display of rugs and blankets outside the nearest shop, caught his eye. He had seen a shepherd wearing such a cloak on his arrival in the northern mountains in April. It was a magnificent heavy woollen garment with a monkish hood. Stephen wanted to see what it felt like to wear. The shopkeeper, quick to notice his interest, had already lifted it down from its hook. Stephen let the man place it round his shoulders. He pulled the hood up, tucking his hair inside as he did so. Then he walked up and down outside the shop. Greek shepherds were much shorter than he was. The full-length cloak barely reached his knees. But the hood was capacious and Stephen's vision was restricted to a narrow segment of pavement in front of his feet. The shopkeeper now ducked into this space, perhaps worried that Stephen might walk away. He stood close, sharing the hood like an umbrella, and talked of the cloak's excellent qualities, its warmth, its resistance to rain, its bargain price. Stephen saw that passers-by had stopped to watch. A crowd was gathering. He struggled out of the cloak hastily. Anyway, it would be no good for biking.

He walked away, disappointed. The thought of buying some sort of souvenir had taken hold. No longer need he be careful about money. If he saw something he liked, he would ask the shop to keep it for an hour, and return with Aunty Vi to buy it. He might even look for presents to give the family. There were many promising little shops in the area. He went from one to another, examining brass pots, goat bells, woven bags, wooden stools, daggers, silver necklaces, earrings, old watches, leather boots, army knapsacks, oil lamps – but nothing was quite right. Many of the shops were shutting for the afternoon siesta. As he passed a restaurant, the sight and smell of food reminded him of his hunger and the need to find the hospital. He decided he must eat, even if he did have to spend his own money on the meal. After all, he was rich. Not only did he have the money in his pocket but he could now use the money he had set aside some weeks ago for his return journey. This was in an envelope which he had put somewhere safe in the van. He entered the restaurant and, from the large containers of food displayed at the counter, chose meat stew with rice and ordered a bottle of wine and a mixed salad to go with it. This was a meal to enjoy, before the arrival of Aunty Vi whose company was bound to be restrictive in one way or another. The meat stew was not as filling as he had hoped, so he asked for a plate of meat balls and a portion of fried potatoes. On the other hand, the bottle of wine was bigger than he had expected and there was still some left when he had finished all the food. So he ordered more bread to help it down.

The bill, when it came, was also bigger than expected. Such a sum would have lasted him three or four days of normal living. He had last counted the money in his pocket about a week ago. He had known he was getting low. That was why he had been hoping to get work with Jake. As he tipped a handful of coins and notes onto the table, he began to have misgivings that he had enough. However, the van, and the return-journey fund, was not far away. This was not a serious situation. On the first count he was 167 drachmas short; on the second, only fifty-five. He remembered having a fifty-drachma note in his back pocket. His hand went to his hip but the movement recalled the moment at the ferry. What had induced him to give away fifty drachmas, and to a kid? He counted the money for the third time, now watched closely by the waiter. This time he was 155 drachmas short.

He looked at the waiter in speculation. What were the chances of being allowed the shortfall? The waiter's expression was answer enough. For one thing, Stephen's appearance did not help on such occasions. For another, he had eaten and drunk a good deal. A more normal-looking foreigner with a more modest bill might well be allowed to run slightly short of money.

Stephen explained, as best he could with the Greek he had learnt, that he had money nearby and would return at once. The waiter did not appear to believe him. Another waiter joined the first. The situation was a little more serious than it had seemed a moment before.

When something similar had befallen his mother, he remembered, she had taken off her watch and left it as guarantee that she would return with cash for the bill. He would leave something – but what? He fingered his bracelet. It had been given to him by a girl who he'd gone out with just before Christmas. Although she had gone off with someone else at a New Year's Eve disco, he had worn the bracelet ever since. He was proud of it. It was more than he had received from a girl before or since. He had always been under the impression that it was silver and worth quite a lot, but now, as he began to unclasp it, he recalled the prices of the silver jewellery he had seen in the shops and began to doubt its value. It was a dull greyish colour, perhaps not silver at all. However, it was surely worth more than his headband or the leather cord tied round one wrist; and, apart from his shoes, pants, T-shirt and jeans, which he could hardly leave, it was all he had to offer. While the waiters watched, he placed the bracelet on the small heap of money on the table and, saying he would return in five minutes, hurried from the restaurant. The waiters were arguing strenuously between themselves but let him go.

Back at the van, Stephen began the search for the safe place in which he had stowed the envelope. He found the cheese he thought he had finished and the pile of unwashed socks. He found a hank of useful rope and the jack and a tyre pressure gauge which might come in handy. He found a packet of disposable razors, a leaving present from Claire. He found an unopened letter from Vicky and five postcards which had been waiting for stamps since June.

It was extremely hot in the van and Stephen suddenly realized that he need not find the envelope. It would be much more sensible to go and collect Aunty Vi and then return with her to pay and pick up the bracelet. He was out of sight of the restaurant. No waiters had followed him. Were it not for the bracelet, which he did not want to lose, he need not return at all. What was 155 drachmas? No more than the restaurant had overcharged for the wine, he thought. He climbed into the driving seat, shut the door as quietly as he could in case there was a waiter hiding nearby, and started the engine.

He had forgotten to ask where the hospital was – and that was the reason why he had parked here in the first place.

For a moment, the complications threatened to overwhelm him. Anger induced by the heat and the hunt was welling up, clouding his ability to think straight. It seemed to him to be Aunty Vi's fault. He began to manoeuvre out of the tight space, trying to sort out what he had to do and in what order. Drive to the hospital. Ask where the hospital was. Avoid the waiters. Get his bracelet back from the waiters. Collect Aunty Vi. From instinct more than from logical thought, he drove off as fast but as quietly as possible. All he wanted to do was to find a shady spot for a lie-down. He thought of the lake on which the town was built. There was shade there and parking space, he remembered. He turned the van towards the lake.

'The nephew has not arrived?'

Violet saw that the doctor was beside her. She looked at her watch. It was nearly half-past five. Tony from Chicago and his famiy had made the time pass pleasantly enough but now her anxiety returned. She laid a hand on the doctor's arm. She did not want him to rush off before she had made contingency plans.

'No,' she answered, 'and if he doesn't, where am I to spend the night? There is someone in my bed. I don't know that I am strong enough to leave the hospital yet. I didn't think I was ready to be released. And the letter and report to my doctor at home? Where are they? And if I must leave, please could you possibly help me find a hotel? And a taxi to reach it?' She realized her voice was sounding querulous.

'All is with the registrar in the office. When your nephew comes, he will help you to the office.' The doctor was looking at his watch. Violet's grip tightened on his arm. She now sympathized with the way the patients and relatives in the ward clung to the doctor's overall whenever he appeared.

'And if he doesn't come today? It's getting rather late.'

'We will make arrangements. Don't worry. There's no problem. If he is not here by seven o'clock, please go to the office. The registrar will give you your papers and the bill and he will telephone for a taxi to a hotel.'

'The bill? But I am not paying the bill. I have insurance.'

'You have insurance. That is good. But you pay the bill.'

'No, no, the insurance company will pay the bill,' said Violet firmly.

'That is not the way. You pay first and then, what is it called, you make the claim. You show your insurance company the bill and they pay you. It is quite simple.'

Violet felt faint. 'But I thought . . .' she began. She let go of the doctor's arm. In fact, she had not thought. She had been confident that her expenses were covered by the insurance policy she had taken out. The mechanics of payment had not entered her head. 'But don't you send the bill to the insurance company?' she asked weakly, already realizing the answer.

'That is not the way,' the doctor said again. 'The bill must be paid now.' His manner was growing a little brusque.

'But I have no money!' Violet took a grip on herself. She must stay calm. 'Of course I have some money,' she said slowly and clearly. 'The holiday was all paid in advance but I brought some spending money. I think I have seventy-five pounds left in traveller's cheques besides whatever I have in my bag – perhaps twenty pounds.' She opened her bag and looked for her wallet. There were three thousand-drachma notes in it and some change. 'How much is the bill?'

'I do not know the bill. It is not my business. The registrar will tell you.' The doctor was moving away. Violet was willing to let him leave. She needed to think this out.

'I shall say goodbye now, Miss Sharpe. I hope that you will soon be finished with the staphylococci and that you have a good journey home.' The doctor held out his hand.

Violet shook his hand absent-mindedly. 'Oh dear. Oh yes, well, thank you very much for all you have done.' She hardly noticed him go.

Tony had been keeping his family informed of the conversation and while Violet sat back and closed her eyes to think, the family discussed what should be done. They decided she must come home with them. It was not good for an old lady in her condition to be kept waiting on a bench. A message could be left for the nephew. They grew excited at the prospect while Violet sat silently beside them, a hand covering her eyes.

How was she to pay the bill? How much could it cost for treatment and five, or was it six, days in hospital. Seventy-five pounds would not be enough. Even if it was – which was most unlikely – she would not be left with anything for the journey home. Stephen might not have enough for the two of them. She would have to get to a bank. Perhaps a Greek bank could ring her bank manager and make some sort of arrangement. This must be possible. Perhaps she could even write an English cheque. She remembered noticing signs on shops for those cards, Access and American Express. She had no such cards but the signs showed there was some sort of currency movement. And wasn't Greece part of the Common Market? Yes, a bank would sort this out. She removed her hand from her eyes. This is not a problem, she thought to herself in imitation of the doctor. But the banks would be shut. Her hand went back to her forehead. If only Stephen would come . . .

She began to feel cross and tired. Stephen should have arrived. If she had been in his position and her Great-aunt Beatrice had needed help, she would have gone at once, the very same day. Really, the young nowadays, no sense of responsibility.

She pulled herself up sharply. She was not Stephen's responsibility. She was no one's responsibility. It was up to her to get herself out of her own muddles. She would get herself home, with or without Stephen. There would be a way. All she needed now was to lie down somewhere and have a rest. She needed a taxi to a hotel. That meant going to the registrar's office. Going to the registrar's office meant dealing with the bill. If she left her passport and the traveller's cheques with the registrar as surety, then he would let her leave. But she would need her passport and the traveller's cheques at the bank. Oh dear! This was too much. She was too tired. In a muddle. She could not think straight. If only Stephen would walk through the door!

While Violet waited, Stephen slept. The van, parked under plane trees between the walls of the old town and the lake, was little cooler than a tin oven. Both front windows were wide open to tempt inside the slight breeze that ruffled the murky green surface of the lake and stirred the drying leaves of the trees. Stephen lay across the two front seats to catch what would have been a through draught had the breeze been stronger. As it was, only flies entered and made him dream of frightful creatures. He was being enveloped in a sticky web of androids. The androids were yellowish-green and oozed a glutinous and stinging liquid from their faces and hands. This they trailed all over his body to pin him down. He struggled feebly and managed at last to free himself from what he knew was a nightmare and not reality. It left him with a longing for home, for a cool bed with clean sheets, a bath with hot and cold taps, and rain falling gently outside a window onto green grass. With these images, he remembered Aunty Vi. He was driving Aunty Vi home. It seemed a good thing to be doing. There would be money, food, comfort; they would stay in hotels on the way, eat well at restaurants. The prospect made him realize that he was tired of roughing it. He had had enough of managing on his own, dealing with people who did not understand him, worrying about money and important pieces of paper. The thought that soon he would be with Aunty Vi, a member of his own family, made him feel relief. It was like carrying something heavy and only realizing how heavy it was when someone took it from you.

He was pleased with this description. He imagined repeating it to Aunty Vi – but that would be an admission of weakness. After all, it was he who was going to look after her, not the other way around. He was coming to her rescue.

And it was high time he started the rescue operation. The sun was well on its way to the horizon. He must have slept two hours or more. Possibly he had drunk quite a lot of wine at lunch. His hand felt for his missing bracelet as he recalled his meal. He owed the restaurant money. He had to find the hospital. He wanted his bracelet back. And where was that envelope of money set aside weeks ago for his journey home? Surely, having been so careful not to break into it, he could not now have lost it. Although with Aunty Vi's purse about to become available he no longer needed the money, he would prefer not to turn up penniless. It would look as though he had not managed on his own. He searched the van again, this time to its deepest layer and obscurest corner. After ten minutes of feverish delving he came to the conclusion that the envelope was no more. It had either fallen out of the van or been stolen.

He would tell Aunty Vi it had been stolen.

Now he *had* to find the hospital. He cleared the driver's seat and settled himself behind the wheel, wondering why he felt suddenly depressed. Certainly the loss of the money was depressing but he knew that this, in itself, was not the cause. He started the engine and then switched it off again. First he must ask the way.

Having been given conflicting instructions by two waiters at a nearby café, Stephen was at last on his way to the hospital and, as he drove through a maze of back streets in what he understood to be the right direction, the reason for his feeling of depression became clear. Up to that moment he had not been fully committed to taking Aunt Violet home. The envelope of money had represented an option. He could have decided one way or the other. He would have had the means to stay longer, find work, and go home on his own. Now there was no question but he must reach the hospital, meet his aunt, become involved with her, her leg, her baggage, her journey.

He felt trapped, a familiar sensation. He always tried to avoid situations which would induce this. He never liked to promise that he would be at a certain place at a certain time. Even if the prompted rendez-vous was only a few hours ahead and just around the corner, he would never say he would definitely be there. How was he to know what mood he would be in when the time came? Something else might have cropped up. For the last six months, he realized, he had never felt trapped. He had been free to do what he wanted when he wanted. Even when he was picking oranges at set times under a stringent foreman, he had not felt trapped because he had needed the money. He knew, too, that the job was temporary. He would not be picking oranges for the rest of his life.

'What are you going to do when you leave school?' He had been asked this, with increasing frequency and pressure, ever since he could remember. He had been asked to choose subjects. Would he rather do woodwork or French? Physics or history? Most of his contemporaries found no difficulty in answering these, to Stephen, unanswerable questions. They were either good at certain subjects or bad at them. Stephen, at that age, was quite good at everything. He was also quite interested in everything. It was like being in an airport with an open ticket. Finally, he was hustled into a choice dictated by the expectations of his parents and teachers. He found himself on a course which concentrated on physics, biology and chemistry. He became less and less interested in physics, biology and chemistry as the subjects became more detailed and difficult. He was not going to become a doctor. For one thing, he did not think he was clever enough to pass even the first stage of exams. For another, his father was a doctor. He gave up any attempt at trying. The harassment this caused made his days more difficult; it also made him more determined not to work. What was the point? Everyone was talking of the unemployment figures. At the same time, they still kept asking what he was going to do when he left school. The answer to him was obvious: go on the dole. While his two best friends, blindly in Stephen's view, chuntered along the course to sixth-form college and university, he made new friends. In the evenings, in pubs, he met bikers in their twenties who lived in a way he admired. Occasionally they would be in work, as mechanics or dispatch riders. One had an HGV licence and sometimes did long-distance driving. Most of the time they drew unemployment benefit. Their conversation he found interesting. They talked of bikes, accidents, and ways to get money from the DHSS. By comparison the conversation of his old schoolfriends, who were now taking A-levels, he found dull and immature. He ceased seeing them.

'But what are you going to *do*?' The question was still being asked. 'You can't get unemployment benefit until you've had a job, and supplementary benefit is not going to support you.' His parents seemed to be wanting him to leave home. He had been on two youth training schemes, one in a small factory which made jigsaw puzzles and one in a cold storage warehouse. His mother had been full of hope at the jigsaw puzzle job. She foresaw a career for him in the development and manufacture of wooden toys. 'They only want cheap labour to sweep up woodshavings,' he had told her but she hadn't believed him. However she had agreed to his decision to leave the cold storage depot. Even she had accepted that this was not the start of a brilliant career in dealing with Europe's butter mountain. On his eighteenth birthday, his parents had rather pointedly stressed the fact of his legal adulthood. 'You are now totally responsible for yourself,' they said, toasting him in home-made champagne. But they still didn't throw him out of the house. They were too worried he would turn to drugs, and by this they meant all drugs, from pot to heroin, ignorant of the fact that he had smoked pot for the last three years. However, they had given him the van – no doubt in the hope he would go away in it, a plan he had talked of for some time. In fact, he had asked for a 950 cc Yamaha; someone he knew was selling one at a reasonable price. But it was the van he was given, and which he had gone away in, and which – a sign to the hospital pulled him back to the present – he was now driving to collect his aunt.

Ever since I had to choose between woodwork and French, he told his aunt in his mind, I've hated being tied down. That's why I feel depressed at losing the envelope. Which was stolen, he added.

The signs led him to a large, red-roofed building set among pine trees on the outskirts of the town. Cars were parked for some distance up and down the road outside. Inside the gates, more cars filled every available space save for one marked, in English and Greek, Emergencies Only. Stephen left the van here and found his way to the main entrance. After half an hour's repeated questioning, he learnt that no Miss Sharpe had been admitted to the hospital, news that banished his depression instantly and replaced it with dismay. More anxious questioning elicited the information that a Miss Sharpe had been registered in the annexe of the hospital, a building which lay on the opposite side of the town. He asked for the address and directions, and returned to the van.

As Stephen edged his way through the crowded streets of the centre, he began to worry about petrol. The gauge, although not wholly reliable, registered empty. He wondered how long the needle had been in that position. It would be awkward to run out of petrol in the middle of the town. It would be hard to find a garage. Besides, he had no money. Each time he changed gear, his eyes went to the needle, but fruitlessly, for it had no further to go downwards and it would hardly start to go up. In fact he was within sight of the annexe when the van faltered and stopped. Ahead he could see the sign with a red cross hanging from a tall old building with grey-louvred shutters, features he had been told to look for.

He managed to push the van to the side of the road and park it at only a slight angle between a lorry and a car. It was not far to walk. He kept his eyes open for garages as he made his way towards the annexe. There was a mechanical-looking workshop down a side-street. Tyres were piled on the pavement but there was no sign of petrol. Down the next side-street he saw a car hire sign. He could ask there when he returned with Aunty Vi.

The annexe stood on the further corner of the next junction. In preparation for meeting his great-aunt, he pulled his headband down over his nose, ran both hands through his hair, shook his head and pushed the band back into place. He noticed that his hands were dusty from manoeuvering the van, so he brushed them against his jeans as he mounted marble steps to the open doorway.

In the waiting-room a hush fell as all eyes turned to the newcomer. Violet at first did not recognize Stephen, although she immediately noticed his arrival. He was clearly a foreigner, one of those travelling students or hippies or whatever they were that one saw everywhere but never really looked at. Violet recalled the photograph she had just been showing her American–Greek friend. If this lad were Stephen, then he had certainly developed into a heavily built young man. His hair had grown much longer and fell in waves below his shoulders. His nose had shrunk – or rather, with his general growth, it was now in better proportion to his face. This was an improvement. But his clothes! Stephen used to wear respectable shirts and trousers, even if the one was not always securely tucked into the other. But this fellow was dressed in rags. There was hardly an inch of trouser not torn or patched. There were gaping holes in his T-shirt. He wore a filthy piece of faintly red cloth low down on his forehead. The whole figure seemed coated in a film of reddish-grey dust. Violet lowered her head hoping that this was not Stephen, however anxious she was for his arrival. What would the Greek family beside her think?

But the Greek family obviously assumed that this was her nephew; Tony was nudging her on one side and Aspasia the other. 'Here he is!' shouted Tony, waving his stick to attract Stephen's attention.

Stephen hesitated for a moment, puzzled by the cheerful signals of an unknown family. Then he noticed that one of them sat with a shoeless foot outstretched. The leg was grossly swollen and purplish-red in colour. Its owner was a white-haired woman sitting with her head bowed and her hands folded in her lap. Was this his great-aunt? Her hair looked right. Aunty Vi did not have one of those permed curly styles that so many old women went in for. Her hair, for as long as he could remember, had been cut short and shaped like an old-fashioned bathing cap. The clothes were right, too. The old woman was wearing an Aunty Vi-ish sort of dress, plain and a kind of blue. The arms, sticking out of the short sleeves, were white, slightly freckled and thin, definitely English arms. He felt a rush of relief.

'Aunty Vi!' he called, and clenched his fists in joyful salute above his head.

Vi looked up and her anxiety vanished as Stephen approached. How cheerful he looked! How young and strong and confident! Never mind his hair and clothes, this was who she had been waiting for. 'Thank heaven,' she breathed as he leant forward and kissed her forehead.

Stephen stepped back awkwardly as Aunty Vi clasped his arm. His kiss on her forehead had taken him by surprise. 'You ready to go?' he asked, finding himself helping the old lady to her feet. 'How's the leg? What did you do? Break it? Mum didn't say on the phone.'

'Carbuncles,' said Vi. 'A ridiculous thing to get.'

'Carbuncles? What's that?'

'People used to get them in the old days when they didn't wash properly. Isn't it shaming? It makes me feel so, well, sluttish. But really, even if I haven't had a bath since I came away – they don't go in for baths in hotels here, do they? – I've had a shower or at least a jolly good wash every day.'

Stephen wondered when it was he had last given himself 'a jolly good wash'. Might he get carbuncles? Or did they not like sea water? He had swum a great deal. 'But what exactly are they?' he asked.

'Oh, horrid little micro-organism things, let's not talk about them. Let's get going. Could you perhaps take my arm? I had a stick but it belongs to the hospital and that reminds me, I'm in a bit of a pickle. I thought I was covered by insurance. At least, I am covered by insurance but what I hadn't realized was that I have to pay the hospital and then claim. And I don't think I have enough. Can you lend me some?'

Stephen was so shaken he could not speak.

Vi, seeing his expression, hurried on. 'Just until I can get to a bank. They'll be shut now, but I can find one first thing in the morning. We'll find a nice hotel.'

'But – um –' Stephen tried to interrupt as Vi continued.

'First help me along to the registrar here and we'll settle up. I must just say goodbye to these nice people.' She turned to Tony and his family and began her farewells.

'But I haven't any money,' Stephen told her loudly.

Vi was saying, 'Yes, isn't he tall. Yes, I'm quite all right now. Thank you so much. Yes, we're on our way.'

Stephen bent his head close to his great-aunt's ear. 'But I haven't any money myself!'

'What, dear? I must just say goodbye to these nice people, they've been so kind to me while I waited.'

'I haven't any money myself, Aunty Vi.' He enunciated the words to the best of his ability.

'No money?' She had heard this time. 'But you must have something! It's only until tomorrow morning, you see. Then I'll get to the bank and arrange things.'

'No money. None. Nothing.'

For a moment they looked at each other blankly, assimilating the situation. Vi's mind was the first to recover. She questioned Stephen to make sure that he really had no money whatsoever, something she found hard to believe. Then she turned to enlist the help of Tony. She asked him to accompany them to the registrar's office and explain their predicament. Although Tony's English was almost half a century old, he understood enough to act as interpreter. As it turned out, the woman in the registrar's office found no difficulty in trusting Violet. She handed over the passport at once and recommended a hotel in the town.

'Is okay,' said Tony. 'She say any time for the money. One week, two week.'

'Oh, we'll be back tomorrow, I'm sure,' said Violet.

'Not tomorrow. Bank is shut Saturday.'

'Oh dear. Well, Monday then.'

They returned to the waiting-room. 'Wasn't that kind,' Vi said to Stephen. 'Aren't people kind. And giving us the name of a hotel. Let's be off, I want to get this wretched leg up on a bed.'

Tony and his daughter insisted on helping them on their way, Tony taking the suitcase, Aspasia Vi's handbag and hold-all, leaving Stephen to support his aunt. The party shuffled down the steps to the street. 'Now where did you manage to park?' Violet asked Stephen.

'Oh, bugger,' said Stephen.

'What dear?'

'Um. Well. A slight problem. Van's just down there. I ran out of petrol.'

Ran out of petrol, Violet repeated to herself when she lay at last on a hotel bed. To have arrived without a *bean* to his name was bad enough, but to have run out of petrol as well. He hadn't even a petrol can in the van. Tony had found one and, old man that he was, had gone marching off to find a garage. If it had not been for Tony . . . How had Stephen managed on his own for six months? How would he manage to get her home? Better if he had not turned up at all. He was going to be a liability, not a help. And there she had been, longing for his arrival, turning him into a knight on a white charger: an inept, filthy, hopeless teenager.

She felt close to tears. Her leg was throbbing wickedly after so long out of bed. She should have overcome her fears, taken Mr Fanshawe's advice, and flown home at once. How silly she was never to fly. The reason had nothing to do with high blood pressure. She would not fly because of something that had happened, how long ago? Over fifty years. She could see the *Times* print, staring up at her from the silver salver on the hall table: R101 airship disaster. October 5th 1930. Crashed at Beauvais.

If she had married him, they would have had eleven years together.

During those eleven years she had never even considered marriage. Had he? It was only after the crash that she began to wonder if he had. He was such a quiet man, so modest, so shy. He had only one leg. He was called Patrick. She had carried this name through her life since the crash like a small child's comforter. She never spoke the name. She was no longer sure what it meant to her now, nor what it had meant to her then.

He had been a friend of her brother Tom.

Violet was in the garden choosing flowers to arrange in the Chinese vase that stood on the hall table. The Chinese vase arrangement was her domain. The flowers in the rest of the house were done by her mother, who considered Violet's flower arrangements odd. Violet had been pleased with the responsibility for the hall flowers. The hall, she thought, was the place where flowers were most often seen. She knew her mother had given her the hall because she thought it was the least important place.

In the trug at her feet lay five sprays of tamarisk, which would make a good background for the roses she was now about to snip from the rambler in front of the house.

She was holding a rose with her left hand and moving the secateurs in her right hand up and down the stem as she looked for the right place to cut. Later it seemed to her that it was at that moment she learnt of Tom's death. Certainly it was that moment which remained vivid. The scrunch of gravel under the bicycle tyres; the tinkle of the bell; turning to see the telegraph boy; dropping the secateurs in the trug among the tamarisk; the rose, uncut, springing back to join its fellows among the virginia creeper; these events remained clear too, but the rest of that day was lost. She no longer had any idea as to how she had learnt the news which the small yellow envelope contained. Had she taken the envelope from the boy and delivered it to her mother? It would have been addressed to her parents so she would not have opened it herself. The envelope, torn open, and the cable folded neatly inside it, now lay among other yellowing papers in an attaché case marked with her father's initials in the bottom drawer of her mother's desk at home.

They had learnt of Tom's death in July. Four months later the war ended. That made it harder; he had survived so long.

Richard, the one who had always intended to be the soldier and who had joined the Army in 1912, had been killed in the first month of the war and in the first battle. He had not had time to come home and say goodbye before leaving for France. As far as Violet remembered, this lack of farewell had not seemed to matter very much at the time. Her parents had talked of the British Expeditionary Force with pride but no alarm. It was as though Richard were going on a normal exercise but one which would take place across the Channel rather than on an English common. Although everyone was talking of 'the war', the words gave a tingle of excitement not terror. It was merely a matter of helping out the French Army. Richard would be home very soon. On August 23rd two British divisions faced six German divisions at Mons. There were 1,600 casualties, one of whom was her brother Richard, and the battle was reported as a great success. The British Army had stopped the German advance, though only for a day. Years later, Violet read somewhere that angels had appeared on the battlefield to help the British. She also read that the Germans had had the mistaken impression that the British were equipped with machine-guns. This had stopped them pushing forward. Violet would have liked to believe in the angels and might well have believed in them had they saved Richard's life. As it was, she merely let herself wonder if God would have favourites. If he did and if he favoured the British, then he might have sown the idea in the German minds that the rifles the British were firing so rapidly and efficiently were machine-guns. But if he had helped the British at Mons, then where was he for the rest of the war?

She did not stop believing in God after Richard's death but she no longer trusted him. After Tom's death she stopped going to church. This was not from lack of faith but from an abundance of tears. The first Sunday after the telegram arrived the tears which had remained tight and dry behind her eyes were suddenly released during the opening hymn. 'Onward Christian Soldiers' was a hymn she had longed to sing ever since but she had never managed to get beyond the middle of the second line. At this point her voice still wavered and she had to clamp her mouth shut and pin her attention on the hassock at her feet. That first Sunday she had been unable to clamp her mouth shut and her mother had led her out of church.

Her mother had not cried with her in the porch. She had stood straight and tall in her navy-blue suit and matching broad-brimmed hat perched at an angle on her coils of greying auburn hair. She had told Violet to pull herself together and to return inside as soon as this was done. Violet had been unable to obey. She had not returned to church either that Sunday or for many Sundays afterwards. Her mother had allowed her to stay at home. She said she did not want Violet making another exhibition of herself.

How was it that her mother could be so controlled herself, and so stern with her youngest child? Looking back, this was puzzling. What would a mother feel whose first-born son was killed when he was twenty and her second four years later? Violet tried to think of her mother simply as a mother, a woman of her generation, but found this impossible. Perhaps if she had become a mother herself she would have been able to understand her better, but she doubted it. Probably she would have understood her even less. Mother had been the most unmotherly of mothers even when they were all young; and when the house emptied and only Violet was left, she had become a cross-tempered invalid who demanded care and attention as vigorously as she resented the need to ask for it. Had Violet loved her? Or had she only longed to be loved by her? Her mother had most certainly loved Richard and Betty. This fact was part of her childhood, something she had grown up knowing. It had not been unduly upsetting because she shared it with Tom.

When Richard was killed, surely her mother had wept? She had no memories of parental grief. But then she had been away at boarding school, only returning at weekends. At school she had acquired the status of heroine. The other girls watched and waited for her to break down. If she sat by herself on the window-seat of the common-room and stared at the laurel hedge outside, the girls withdrew with tactful whispers. To them it was the height of Byronic romance to be mourning for an older brother killed in battle. But Violet was not thinking of Richard. Her thoughts were all with Tom, who had begun talking of enlisting.

How could her parents have allowed Tom to join up? Certainly they had not encouraged him to do so, unlike other families in the fervour of patriotism, but they had not forbidden it. In any case, Tom had needed no encouragement. Would she herself, had she been in the position to do so, have forbidden it? Not at the time. Kitchener's finger pointed at them all. She, like everyone else, was more than ready to do everything for King and Country. She could do nothing. Tom would do it for her.

When she stared out of the common-room window she was not mourning for Richard but mourning for Tom. In the autumn of 1914, she was one of the few who knew that the war across the Channel was more than an exercise on an English common. She had lost one brother. She would lose another.

Tom joined the Army and became a pilot in the Royal Flying Corps. He had wanted to fly ever since Uncle

Edmund had taken him to Margate to watch for Blériot. For days after that, he had talked of little else but the sight of the small monoplane appearing through the clouds and landing in the very field where the crowds had gathered. He began to read everything he could find on aircraft. In the holidays he made balsawood models of the latest designs. 'One day,' he promised Violet, 'I'll take you up in the air.' Up in the air sounded intoxicating when uttered by sixteen-year-old Tom to twelve-year-old Vi.

A knock on the door made her stir. She was momentarily puzzled by her surroundings, then she collected her thoughts. 'Now I am eighty-six and I'm lying in bed because I will not fly. A hospital? No, a hotel.'

Stephen's head appeared at the door.

Patrick had been a pilot too.

Stephen was driving her home.

'Are you hungry?' Stephen asked .

'Is it late? I expect you are. I've been having a nice rest.'

'It's after eight. A clock struck. I ought to go back to the place I had lunch. I owe them a bit of money. I left my bracelet. As, what's it called? Guarantee?'

Bracelets were worn by women. 'Surety,' she said. And more incompetence, not being able to pay a bill. But neither had she at the hospital. 'We'll have to think about this money business,' she continued. 'Can you see my handbag? Is it on the dressing-table? Come in and shut the door behind you, there are people looking in.'

Counting the money in his great-aunt's wallet as instructed, Stephen felt awkward. It seemed a very personal thing to do and he didn't think he knew her well enough. 'You have 3,305.' With seventy pounds' worth of traveller's cheques, it was almost as much as he had put aside (and lost) for his return journey.

'And how much is that in English money?'

'Twenty quid or so.'

Quid. 'Well that will see us through until we get to the

bank on Monday. I did pay that nice Greek–American for the petrol, didn't I? Really, he was so kind . . .'

'Will you be getting up? To come and eat?'

Violet would have liked to talk to Stephen about the conversation she had had in the hospital waiting-room but she accepted his interruption. Food was important to growing boys. 'Is it far?' she asked.

'No. Just down the street. It's the nearest one to this hotel in any case.'

'I'll just have to manage it.' She carefully lifted the sheet that covered her legs.

Stephen moved towards the door.

'You wanted to know what carbuncles are,' said Vi. 'Come and look at these.' It would be nice to have some sympathy. Two of the swellings looked ready for a further squeezing session with cotton wool. But perhaps she should not have inflicted the sight on Stephen. He glanced back at her leg and made a sound in imitation of someone being sick.

'I'm not *that* interested, thanks,' he said with a laugh. 'I'll be downstairs – there's a telly room, sort of. I'll be in there.'

The image of Violet's leg lingered in his mind, despite his attempts to concentrate on watching television. A talent contest was in progress. There was a panel of judges, each enclosed in a box done up like a Christmas parcel, and various lights flashed on or off to the sound of buzzers as a line of costumed children marched past. He tried to work out what talent might be the subject of competition, in order to dispel the sight of a parchment-white and skeletal leg invaded from the knee down by angry red puffballs exuding yellow pus. He had been shocked. He would have been shocked to be shown Aunty Vi's leg at the best of times. But then, she would not have shown it to him were it not for the carbuncles. He would make sure that he never became that old. He must make sure he never got carbuncles. Were they catching?

He turned away from the television and went upstairs to have a shower.

*

Patrick was a pilot too, thought Violet as she dabbed at her leg with cotton wool. *I only need the left one.* That was much later. Her first memory of Patrick was watching him race Tom across the tennis court and down towards the pond.

The three of them had been sitting on the garden seat outside the windows of the morning-room.

The kiss of the sun for pardon,
The song of the birds for mirth;
One is nearer God's heart in a garden
Than anywhere else on earth.

The verse was carved on the back rail of the wooden seat which now faced her small white cottage from its position beneath a eucalyptus tree. This tree had become an embarrassment. It had outgrown the patch of lawn. She had been meaning to have it cut down for some years but she had had difficulty in finding someone willing to do the job. One specialist firm of tree-fellers had given a ridiculously high estimate. An odd-job man in the village who sometimes helped her out had been promising to do it and would no doubt go on promising for years. Perhaps she could ask Stephen. Perhaps, after the journey, Stephen would become someone of whom she could ask such favours. She would pay him for the trouble, of course. It would be good to be able to call on someone young, a member of her family. They did not live so far away. It was only twenty minutes or so by car. Stephen and his family lived in a house built in the 1960s on what had been the tennis court.

She could see the two young men in uniform running across the grass, leaping the white lines. Tom had brought this new friend home on leave. Patrick Fitzpatrick came from Ireland.

'Don't trust him, Vi. He's only fighting for us now to get practice for fighting against us later.'

Violet didn't understand what Tom meant by this. She sat on the seat with them, trying to follow their conversation which seemed to be composed mainly of the exchange of initials: BEs, FEs, REs, SEs. Even the sentences free of initials were puzzling until they explained that pups, camels and dolphins were not animals but aircraft. She was sixteen and sat on the seat trying to stop trembling.

She wanted Tom's friend to notice her but not her trembling. She wanted Tom to realize that she was now grown up, and struggled to find a way to enter the conversation which would demonstrate this fact. Suitable phrases eluded her. The two young men, although ostensibly addressing her and explaining wings, squadrons, units and corps for her benefit, were in fact ignoring her. To them she was still a child. When Tom at last paid her attention, he jumped to his feet.

'Look, Vi's shivering. Come on, let's show Patrick our boat.' He pulled her to her feet. 'Race you,' he said to them both. Vi could have become a child again and joined in the race. But she hesitated and returned to the seat. She was not cold. She watched Tom and Patrick race across the garden and disappear.

The next time she saw Patrick, he had only one leg and Tom was dead.

It was early in 1919. Her mother laid aside a black-bordered letter and threaded a napkin into her napkin ring. 'That is from Mrs Caulfield. She tells me that Patrick Fitzpatrick is in Heathfield Nursing Home. I think I shall visit him.'

At the other end of the table, her father lowered the newspaper. Violet saw that he had no idea who Patrick Firzpatrick was. Her mother explained without using Tom's name. Violet decided at once that she wanted to see Patrick too. He would be able to answer questions.

'May I come with you?' she asked.

Mother and Father exchanged looks. Her father raised his paper, so it was Mother's decision.

'I'm glad you feel like getting out but I think perhaps that this is not a suitable occasion.'

If Betty, who was away at the time, had wanted to visit the nursing home, they would not have hesitated to let her. She had nursed wounded soldiers and so was inured to distressing sights. She was also used to being out in the world and was now engaged to be married to a soldier she had nursed in London. This was perhaps the more important reservation in her parents' minds. Violet suspected that they did not want to run the risk of her meeting and marrying a wounded soldier too. It was possible they did not want her to marry at all. She was eighteen. Since Tom's death six months previously she had not been out and her mother had not encouraged her to extend or accept any invitations. The only social occasions that had taken place in the house were her mother's weekly bridge parties to which Violet was invited only when it was necessary to make up a four. This absence of social life suited her. She hardly noticed the days going by, so deep was her grief.

'It's not that I want to go out,' she said. 'But I would like to talk to someone who knew – who was with . . .' She struggled for a moment. 'Patrick was there. He could tell us how it was.' She glanced at her mother and saw that this was understood. Her mother, as much as she herself, needed proof of Tom's death, something more than the cable. They both wanted to know what he had been doing, what he had been thinking, what he had been saying before he went up in the air for the last time. Had he been thinking of them? Patrick might have photographs, even a message.

Her mother laid a hand on Violet's shoulder as she left the breakfast table. 'Be ready at three o'clock. We'll go today.'

'Take the motor. I'll send a note to Wesley.' This was her father's way of showing his understanding. Usually he was miserly over the use of the car. Or was it jealousy? He liked to drive it himself. If Mother was going somewhere on her own, then Wesley had to be called in. He thought Wesley punished the engine. 'He has hard hands,' he would complain. 'It is not a horse, dear,' Mother would reply. 'Wesley drives beautifully. Besides, he understands engines.' Wesley could always start the car even when it was wet. Father could not. Many a time, while shivering under the black and red travelling rug in the back seat and waiting for Father to manhandle life into the motor-car, Vi and Mother wished fervently that Wesley always drove.

At three o'clock Wesley brought the silver-grey Triumph round from the stables to the front door and helped Violet and her mother climb into it. They did not speak at all on the way to the nursing home, but as they drew near Mother laid her gloved hand on Violet's arm and left it there for a moment. The gesture filled Vi with emotion, as had the hand on her shoulder at breakfast-time. Her mother did understand what she felt, and felt much the same. She determined to be as collected and controlled as the straight-backed, expressionless woman beside her. She stiffened her own back and turned to look at the landscape.

They were passing a park. Fat white sheep with black faces were browsing vividly green grass. The expanse of green was broken every so often by an oak tree whose leafless branches made a shape like a black-lace fan against a pearl-grey sky. Violet thought: I had forgotten how utterly beautiful the world is.

They drove through a village where people turned to stare, and a few old men sitting on a bench touched their caps. Wesley hooted the horn at a butcher's boy on a bicycle in the middle of the road. The boy was holding his knees out at right angles and seemed to be wobbling on purpose. It was some time before he moved out of the way, and when at last they overtook him, Violet saw that he was laughing. His expression made her smile.

'Just imagine,' said her mother as they turned into a dark driveway beyond the village, 'I used to come here for parties when I was your age.'

The drive led through thickets of holly, laurel and spindly

firs. 'How overgrown it has become,' sighed Mother. 'And what have they done to the house?' Ahead stood a grey-stone turreted building. 'It used to be covered in wonderful creepers. And they've changed its shape, added on bits. Bathrooms, I suppose – but why on earth in the front, for all the world to see the pipes? What a sad mess.'

She continued to bemoan the changes as they were led through the house by a young woman. Violet was staggered by the appearance of the young woman, who could not be much older than herself. Her hair was cut short and her skirt barely covered the calves of her legs. She was not wearing uniform so was not a nurse. What was she? Her manner was unusual too. She was talking with her mother in a way that Violet found hard to pin down. Was it overfamiliar? Too loud? Too cheerful? Violet decided it was not too anything. It was a way of talking that she herself would like to emulate.

'And this is where we should find Patrick,' said the young woman, throwing open a final door.

'Gracious me, this is where we danced,' said her mother, staring into the long, high-ceilinged room. She was looking into the past and saw perhaps chandeliers and swirling couples. Violet was looking at the present and saw a roomful of bandaged men sitting slumped in chairs as various as might be found at an auction sale: leather armchairs, canvas deckchairs, moquette sofas. It was not the bandages or the lethargic attitudes of the men that brought home to her the injuries suffered by these survivors, but their silence. The huge room was crowded. At the far end there were two playing table-tennis. The strains of a music-hall song came from a gramophone in a distant corner. There were groups playing cards, and others with heads bent in conversation. Yet these sounds did not dispel the hushed atmosphere; rather, they emphasized it.

'Is Patrick here?' called their guide brightly. She led them down the room, nodding and smiling to the men they passed. One or two responded with a word. Most, if they looked up at all, gazed at them with unseeing eyes.

Patrick was playing cards near the gramophone. He noticed their approach and, after a second's hesitation, recognized them. His hands went to the arms of his wheelchair as though he would get to his feet. 'Mrs Sharpe,' he said. 'And, and.'

He had forgotten her name?

'Miss Sharpe,' he said as she said, 'Violet.'

'Please don't get up,' said Mother and then stopped. Violet had seen at once that the chair he was sitting in with his legs covered in a faded tartan rug was a wheelchair. There was a moment's silence, then both Patrick and Mother spoke at once.

'How jolly decent of you to come.'

'How are you, Patrick?'

Violet stood unhappily by, knowing that the visit was a mistake. It wasn't at all decent of them to come. They had come not for the sake of Patrick but for themselves and Tom. Her mother so far had said the wrong thing each time she had opened her mouth. Patrick could obviously not get up. And one did not ask a man with a thin, grey face sitting in a wheelchair how he was. Violet wished the young woman had stayed with them. She would have made it easy for them. But she had disappeared as soon as they had found Patrick.

'Will you sit down? Let me introduce you to –' He turned to the other card-players.

'We don't want to disturb your game.'

'Oh, we only play while we wait and hope for such marvellous disturbances. Can we make room on the sofa?'

The three other card-players refused the invitations to stay exactly where they were and gave up their seats for the visitors.

'This place is overcrowded. It was full before Christmas but they are still sending people down from London. We used to have a room where we could entertain our visitors. It's got six beds in it now.'

Mother began to tell Patrick how she had known the

nursing home in the old days. Violet almost relaxed; surely this was a foolproof subject. She stole glances at Patrick, trying to see in him the young man who had made her tremble so inexplicably. It was impossible; only the soft Irish voice that had charmed her before was the same. He did not look at her. She wondered why he was in a wheelchair and tried not to gaze at the tartan rug. She had heard of soldiers who had had both legs blown off yet survived. Nanny Burton had told her this. Did the tartan rug look thin, as though it covered nothing? She willed her eyes to the fans of cards laid on the table in front of her.

'And can you imagine, in this very room we used to dance,' she heard her mother saying.

Violet wanted to jump to her feet and whisk her mother home. As it was, she remained rigidly in her chair, wishing she could think of a way to enter, and change, the conversation. *Nanny Burton says that – Remember how you raced – How exactly was Tom killed?*

'Were you playing whist or bridge?' She had spoken. That was her voice. She had interrupted her mother's monologue. Even if the words had come out too suddenly and too loudly, she had managed it.

She looked up. Patrick had turned towards her. She saw that he understood exactly why she had spoken so abruptly and that he was grateful. 'Whist,' he said. 'I remember when I stayed with you that you and your mother gave us a most tremendous thrashing at bridge and I've never dared play since.'

Suddenly it was easier. The talk lingered over card-games and then somehow progressed to the exorbitant price of butter. But there it stuck. Patrick's 'us' was the nearest they got to talking of Tom. Soon Mother said it was time they left. Patrick hoped they would come again.

'The poor boy. Only one leg and he was such an athlete.' They were in the car.

'Are you sure? Could you see?' Violet was startled but relieved.

'Mrs Caulfield told me in her letter. They had hoped to save it but it was no good. They amputated only a month or so ago.'

'I wish you had told me before.' She would have been spared her dreadful imaginings.

Her mother thought for a moment. 'Perhaps I should,' she admitted.

After this visit to the nursing home, there was a marked change in their relationship. Mother seemed to accept that her younger daughter was no longer a little girl. Violet became more confident in herself and less confident in her mother. The next time she visited, she went on her own.

Stephen found his aunt waiting for him in the entrance lobby of the hotel.

'Sorry. I decided to . . .' But he wouldn't say he had taken a shower as a precaution against carbuncles. 'Change,' he said.

Vi glanced at his clothes which looked identical to those he had been wearing. How could she tactfully suggest that he buy some new ones?

'We might look at the shops tomorrow if I'm up to it. I must buy myself a stick of some description.'

'You could buy a shepherd's crook.'

'Would I be able to lean on it? In the meantime, can I lean on you?'

Stephen gave her his arm and they made their way slowly out of the hotel, through a small public garden and into a wide street. The pavements were crowded.

'I hope it's not too far.' Violet was walking even more slowly.

Stephen became conscious for the first time that his aunt's limp was caused by pain. He thought guiltily of the distance he had expected her to walk from the hospital to the van. It was Tony who had suggested that she wait in the hospital until a canful of petrol had been found so that Stephen could bring the van to the door. 'Just to the bottom of the hill,' he said. 'Would you like to rest?' But there was nowhere for her to sit down.

'Better keep going. In fact, it's the change of angle that's worst. Once I'm walking it's not so bad.'

Stephen was aware of the looks they were getting from passers-by. They must make an ill-assorted pair. Aunty Vi's head barely reached his shoulder. On her swollen foot she was wearing the best sock he had been able to find for her. 'It must be horrid,' he said.

Violet was touched by the tone of voice. Were it not for the sloppy enunciation it might almost have been Tom speaking. It reminded her that Stephen was part of her family, and this gave her comfort.

'We ought to telephone your mother this evening. She'll be glad to know you've found me.'

There was a telephone they could use in the restaurant. The waiters were all smiles now. Stephen thought that this was due not so much to his return as to the respectable age and appearance of his companion. They fussed all over her. The menu was brought with a flourish. Not only was the flimsy nylon cover whisked away from the table but also the linen cloth beneath. Fresh ones were laid with ceremony. Various bottle of wine were brought for her inspection but she produced from her handbag a foil-covered sheet of pills in order to explain she was on a course of antibiotics and must not drink. Stephen drank beer. Although he had eaten unusually well at midday, he found he was able to manage a generous helping of chicken casserole and rice. So did Aunty Vi. She said she had not had much to eat in the hospital. 'There's nothing wrong with my appetite, I'm glad to say.' They talked of the journey home. Aunty Vi wanted to know which way he planned to go and how long it might take. If they were going through Italy, would they be able to visit Rome? She would love to see Rome again. And which way would they take through the Alps? Might they be near Chamonix where she had a friend?

'What fun it will be,' she said.

Stephen, listening to his aunt's hopes and wishes, did not think it would be fun at all. 'Van's not too – well, it's fine but . . . We'd better just go the shortest way back. Do it in three days.'

'Three days! Good heavens!'

'Not counting the crossings. Ferry to Brindisi and the Channel.'

'What about booking? Won't the ferries be full?'

Stephen hadn't thought about this. 'What's the date?' he asked. On his own he would just turn up at the port and wait till he got on a ferry. He had the van to sleep in. Aunty Vi would not sleep in the van.

'I've lost track,' said Vi, rummaging in her bag for her diary. She leafed through its pages. 'August 10th,' she read. 'Meet at Gloucester Hotel for coach. That's the date I left England. It took us five days to drive down to Greece. I don't see how we can do it in three.'

'Which way though?'

'Through Belgium, Germany, Austria, Yugoslavia –'

'Far longer,' put in Stephen but Vi was continuing.

'– very pleasant. We stayed at some very nice hotels on the way. Let's see, the first weekend, 16th and 17th, we were in north-eastern Greece. Yes, Lake Kerkini on 16th. Squacco heron, Ardeola ralloides, marvellous, so many of them! Have you been to those lakes? You'll have to tell me all about your time out here.'

Stephen brought her back to the point and established that as Vi had gone into the clinic on Monday, then it was now Friday August 29th.

'The others will be on their way home now,' said Vi. 'Yes, we were due to get back to Victoria on the evening of the 1st.'

'We've got to wait here till Monday, for the bank. That's the 1st, isn't it? I suppose it will still be crowded. Maybe we'd better go to a travel agent tomorrow and book. Might get away in the afternoon so we could book a crossing for Monday night.'

'So we might be back in England the following weekend? That's the 6th, 7th. We ought to have a rough date to tell Elizabeth.'

'Okay, we'll tell her the 6th or 7th. Do you want to talk to her, or shall I?'

Violet did not want to move from the table until she must, so Stephen made the call. The telephone was on a shelf between the serving counter and their table. He was lucky and got through the third time he dialled. He had to shout, which was embarrassing. The whole restaurant was listening.

'Mum? Steve. Petropolis. Yeah. Yeah. Fine. Great. Carbuncles. *Carbuncles*. Fine. Great. Yeah. The weekend . . . no, not this weekend, *next* weekend . . .'

Violet called, 'Tell her the date.'

'What was the date?' asked Stephen.

'The *sixth*.'

'The sixth,' Stephen told the phone.

'Or the seventh,' called Aunty Vi.

'Or the seventh. No, we're still in Greece. No, not tomorrow, Monday. Monday. No, I said *next* weekend. The sixth. Sixth or seventh. Okay. Yeah. Great. Bye.'

He returned to the table feeling the need for another beer. Would Aunty Vi think of asking him? Could he ask her? A great-aunt was not like a parent. What he would like to do was borrow a thousand drachmas so that he could go off on his own for a drink somewhere.

'How do they know how much that cost?' his aunt was asking.

'It's on a meter. Clicks up like a taxi. They'll put it on the bill. Look, Aunty Vi –' He thought of her as Aunty Vi, but when he said it aloud he felt foolish. 'You'll go back to the hotel now, won't you? I mean, I'll take you, of course, but I thought I'd go for a bit of a wander round. Could I borrow some cash, do you think?'

Had she taken this in? She was waving her arm and looking for a waiter. 'Yes,' she said, 'I am ready for bed now.

We'll settle up and go back to the hotel. What, dear?'

'I'll have a wander round. Could I, do you think, borrow some cash?'

'No, dear, I'll pay for this, of course. I wouldn't *dream* of letting you –'

'But – oh shit.' He would have another go on the way back to the hotel. The waiter was now at the table, totting up the bill. As Aunty Vi counted notes, the waiter produced Stephen's bracelet from the pocket of his white jacket. Stephen put the bracelet on his wrist. At least he'd got that back.

With two hundred drachmas in his pocket, which was all that Aunty Vi had given him, Stephen took himself off to find some life in the town. He tried a bar where there were pool tables but the wrong kind of music. He gazed at posters outside a cinema, but he wanted a drink not Clint Eastwood. In the end he found himself down by the lake where there was a group of young foreigners sitting at a café. Without too much difficulty he joined them. Although they weren't the type he would seek out in normal circumstances, they would do as company while he drank his beer. They were a mixed bunch of students, German, Dutch, French and English, and their conversation was a reviving contrast to Aunty Vi's.

One of the English girls had been travelling in a van not unlike his with her Dutch boyfriend. They exchanged experiences and place names. Stephen took a certain pleasure in the cachet the greater length of his stay gave him. He'd been away from England for six months; they, for only six weeks.

'So what do you do about the tax thing,' the girl asked him, 'if you've been here since April?'

'What tax thing?' asked Stephen.

'Oh that business about not being allowed to keep a car in the country longer than six months.'

Stephen did not know what she was talking about. He

didn't want to admit his ignorance but, on the other hand, he ought to find out what she meant. He drank deeply from his glass of beer.

The girl called across to her Dutch boyfriend. 'Remember that couple we met at the border? The teachers trying to leave Greece in their car? What was their problem exactly? Come and sit over here and tell Steve.'

She had guessed he knew nothing. While the Dutch boyfriend told him a long story about the English couple who had had such difficulty because their car had been in Greece for nine months, Stephen tried desperately to work out the exact length of his own stay. He would have to check the entry stamp in his passport the minute he got back to the hotel. The story was long and involved. The couple had been faced with the choice of giving up their car or paying a very large sum of tax and they could afford to do neither. After two attempts at the Yugoslavian border and long waits in offices in Thessaloniki and Athens, they had finally managed to leave from Patras, thanks to fresh passports.

Shit, thought Stephen. If he were to be turned back at Igoumenitsa with Aunty Vi . . . Would she pay the tax for him? Four or five hundred pounds, the English girl suggested, on a van like his. Twice as much as it was worth! Aunty Vi would never do it. Fresh passport? How did one get a fresh passport, for Christ's sake? He stood up. He must get back to the hotel immediately.

He strode up the hill to the hotel muttering to himself as he counted on his fingers: April, May, June, July, August, September. Six. But it was only the beginning of September. No, even better, it was still August. Monday was the 1st. He knew he had left England in March; on St Patrick's Day, the 17th, the day on which Pepper the family dog had been born many years before. There'd been talk of calling the dog Paddy. March, April, May, June, July, August. Six. No, even worse, seven, for it would be September when they left. How long had he and Jake taken to drive to Greece? One week? Three weeks? He could not remember. His passport would tell him.

Back in his hotel room he remembered that he had handed in his passport, with Aunty Vi's, at the desk on arrival. It would be given back tomorrow. He clattered down the stairs to the lobby where there was an elderly man on duty. Stephen took one look at him and knew it was pointless to ask such a man anything, let alone for the return of a passport. He returned upstairs and eventually fell asleep to dream of the bomb's aftermath. The nightmare followed its usual pattern and he woke in the morning with the familiar feeling of depression. He hauled a sheet over his head, despite the morning heat, and went back to sleep.There was nothing to wake up for – only trouble.

Vi had woken early. There was a small balcony outside her room on which stood a circular metal table and two chairs. At this hour of the morning the sun was pleasant and she had made herself comfortable, with a pillow on one chair for her leg and a blanket on the other to sit on. This made up for the several broken plastic strings of the chair seats. There were many people about in the street below and the traffic was brisk. Vi had been watching the movement with interest until the hands of the clock in the public garden opposite reached eight o'clock.

'This won't do,' she said and reached for her handbag. Instead of idling away the time like this, she must do her accounts. First, she emptied her purse on the table and counted the money. She had 695 drachmas left. This was something of a shock. Only yesterday evening Stephen had counted and there had been three thousand and something. She tried to recall his voice saying the figure. (How like Tom he was – but only in certain ways.) She had counted the money herself while she waited at the hospital. How much had the petrol cost? Then there was yesterday's meal and the telephone call. And after that enormous meal, Stephen had asked to borrow money for a *drink*! As though he hadn't had enough already. *Two* bottles of beer with the meal.

Would she have to control him? Did he have a weakness for drink? How difficult this would be. It wasn't as if she were his mother. Perhaps she should not have given him any money last night. But she knew she couldn't have refused him. He was being so kind to her. And, in spite of his amazing appearance, he really was quite well-mannered and charming. It could be no fun at all for him to look after an old woman like her. Of course he wanted to go out and meet people of his own age. And you can't go anywhere nowadays without spending money.

She found her notebook and pen and drew a long division sign. If there were 160 drachmas in a pound, then how much were 200 drachmas worth? She filled in the figures but saw at once that she had only given Stephen a little more than a pound. This meant that the money she had left was worth very little too; and it had to last until Monday. No, she had the traveller's cheques, seventy pounds' worth. She hoped the hotel might be willing to cash these for her.

The next thing to work out was how much money she should get from the bank on Monday. She began jotting down items and estimates: hospital, hotels for ten nights (to be on the safe side), ferries (two), petrol, food. It was extraordinarily difficult to estimate how much these things would cost. Only the hospital bill she knew with any certainty. She had thought the total sum needed might come to five hundred pounds or so. It was beginning to look as though a thousand might not be enough.

Did she have a thousand pounds in her current account? She liked to keep the balance around this figure but she rather thought it might have gone down while she was away. Various standing orders would have been paid in her absence.

One thousand pounds! The enormity of her holiday's extra expense sank in. And all because of a few carbuncles! Elsie was right. She should not go on holiday abroad at her age. No, her neighbour was not called Elsie. Elsie wore a cap and apron and had a pointed nose and sharp eyes. She was always spying on the children and reporting their misdemeanours to Nanny Burton. Those days were easily recalled. But the cottage she had locked up a few weeks ago was a blur. What was it like? And what was her neighbour's name? Elsie, Ethel, Ivy, Olive, Elspeth, Edna. . .

Not Ivy. Ivy sent her Christmas cards from Chamonix. What fun it would be to call on her. Violet found her address book in her handbag to check that Chamonix was Ivy's most recent home. Yes, there it was: Apartement 15, 173 Rue des Alpes, La Mollard, Chamonix. No telephone number unfortunately. However, Ivy wasn't the kind to be put out by the unannounced arrival of a friend, even if she had not seen that friend for –

Perhaps it was rather a long time.

She had become friends with Ivy at the nursing home. The second time she had visited Patrick, on this occasion without her mother, she had been called into Ivy's room for a cup of tea just as she was about to leave.

'It's such a relief to talk to someone young, healthy and *female,*' Ivy told her.

Knowing Ivy made being female an entirely different matter.

Ivy's mother was the matron of the nursing home. Ivy was only helping there temporarily while more staff were found. Under normal circumstances, she lived in a little flat in Holborn with her elder sister. They were both studying at art school. Ivy had decided that photography interested her more than painting. After her final examinations in the summer she would become a photographer.

Violet, at that time, could only nod and murmur 'how interesting'. Everything that Ivy said or did was a revelation.

'You simply must come and stay with me in London,' said Ivy. She was due to return there the following week. Extra staff had been found.

Violet by now had had tea with Ivy on three occasions.

But for the chance to listen to Ivy, she might not have visited Patrick so often.

'Oh, how I wish I could!' she said.

'But whyever can't you?'

'My parents . . . Staying in London on my own! They'd never let me.'

'Then I shall come over and have tea with you and I will tell them to let you.'

Violet laughed at this intoxicating assurance. It was extremely unlikely that her parents would approve of her friend, for a start. That they would give Vi permission to stay with her in London was beyond the realms of possibility. However, the idea of introducing Ivy to her parents was appealing. A meeting would show her friend how entirely different her own circumstances were and how impossible it would be for her ever to lead an Ivy kind of life.

The meeting was arranged. Ivy came to tea and was an immediate success with Father. They talked about Box Brownies and Leicas, lighting and exposures. Father showed Ivy his album of butterfly photographs taken with his plate camera. Ivy told Father that Patrick had been taking photographs of icicles. She thought Patrick could earn a living as a photographer. He was extremely talented, she said. It was something he could do. 'You don't need two legs for taking photographs,' she said with a laugh. Mother blenched. He had all that war experience, too. Apparently he was passionate about airships and had ideas about the civilian possibilities of aerial photography using airships rather than planes. It could help town planning and agriculture.

Vi and Mother handed cups of tea and scones and listened. Patrick had never said a word to Vi about these interests.

'What a lot of nonsense,' said Mother after Ivy's departure. 'As though that poor young man will be able to do anything useful again –'

'Whyever not?' asked Father crossly.

They argued for some time about Patrick's chances of earning a living. Vi realized that the argument really concerned their differing reactions to Ivy. Mother disapproved of Ivy, that was clear. It was equally clear that Father approved. No mention had been made by either girl of a possible visit to London. A few days later, a thank-you letter arrived addressed to Mother. It must have been well worded for Mother responded more magnanimously to Father's continuing allusions to 'Violet's young friend'. Another week passed and then Ivy issued her invitation. Again it was addressed to Mother. It begged Mrs Sharpe to spare Violet for a few days. 'My sister and I would like her to accompany us to a concert being held in aid of wounded servicemen.' At this, Mother succumbed.

When the time came, only Ivy and Vi went and it was not to a concert, though a charitable concert was advertised for that evening, but to a *party*. And when the few days were up, Violet returned home with her hair bobbed.

She should shampoo her hair. It was in a dreadful mess. The hands of the clock were approaching nine. It was high time she got moving. Stephen would probably have had his breakfast by now.

But Stephen did not have breakfast that day or on any of the days they stayed in that hotel. Vi was at first alarmed by his staggering ability to sleep until midday. Then she came to accept it, only hoping that when at last they started on their journey home he would get up early. She would make sure he did. Till then, there was no reason why he should not sleep the entire day.

The stick which she had bought herself on Saturday evening made her independent of Stephen's arm. In any case, there was a steady, though slow, improvement in her leg. On Sunday she had managed to walk as far as the museum, where she had spent at least an hour. On Monday she had gone to the bank first thing in the morning. She had spent two hours there while attempts were made to telephone her bank manager. Eventually she had spoken to him herself and made the situation clear. A bank draft for a thousand pounds would be telexed at once. She did not understand exactly what this meant but it sounded suitably expeditious. On Tuesday morning she went to the bank. The money was not yet through. She went again on Wednesday.

On Thursday Stephen became as anxious as she. He was again worried about the date. It was something to do with the van. The previous Saturday, when he had finally emerged from his room, he had seized his passport, which the hotel manager had handed back to her in the morning. His date of entry was important and the reason for this, as far as she could understand from his garbled explanation, was that he was not allowed to stay in the country for more than six months. He had arrived in Greece on March 24th. He had to leave before September 24th.

'Unless', he said on Thursday as they ate a picnic lunch on Vi's balcony, 'they count it in weeks. You know, like six lots of four. Where's your diary?'

Violet rummaged in her handbag. 'I don't think they would do that.'

'It might give us more time. Chuck it here.'

Violet handed him the diary. Chuck it here, she repeated to herself. 'Wouldn't it give us less?' she suggested.

'Today's the 4th.'

'I'm sure we'll be quite all right,' said Vi with as much conviction as she could muster. 'We have twenty days. Plenty of time.'

'Twenty days in Greece is *nothing*,' said Stephen. 'I *know* how long things take here.'

'The bank says the money will definitely be through tomorrow.'

'Yeah, and that's what they said on Monday and Tuesday and Wednesday, didn't they?'

'But twenty days! It simply cannot take that long.'

Stephen, with a moistened and grimy finger, was turning the diary's pages as he counted the weeks.

Vi pointed out that all the months were printed together at the beginning and wouldn't this make counting easier? The sight of Stephen thumbing through the pages of her diary made her feel uncomfortable. Not that the few engagements pencilled within were in the least private . . .

But Stephen paid no attention. 'Twenty-two, twenty-three, we're into the twenty-fourth week. Six fours are twenty-four.' He looked up at her with a stricken face.

'I said it would be less that way,' said Violet smugly.

'We don't *want* it to be less!'

She had irritated him, she could see. 'They would never count six months like that. I am quite sure they mean six calendar months. Perhaps we should find some sort of office where we can ask? The AA, for instance.'

'The AA!' Stephen jumped to his feet, making the table clatter.

'Where are you going? You haven't finished this nice salami. Do you know where the AA office is?'

''Course there's not an AA office here.'

No doubt he was thinking she was a foolish old woman. 'There are AA offices in France,' she said. 'I know that for a fact.' Her voice was sharp and his expression changed. Perhaps he now thought she could be right and that there might be an AA office in the town.

'I'm not going to any office,' he said at last. 'That's the last thing we want to do.'

'Whyever not?'

'They start asking questions. You don't ever want to go to offices.'

Was there, wondered Violet, some other reason for Stephen's anxiety? She recalled newspaper stories of young men arrested for smuggling. 'Come and sit down again,' she said, her hand on his chair. 'We must finish the salami, otherwise it will start to smell dreadfully.'

Edith! Her neighbour was called Edith. The name had suddenly surfaced like a fish rising. What strange tricks memory played.

After lunch Stephen had gone off on his own and Violet lay on her bed with a two-day-old copy of *The Times* in her hand. She was doing the crossword and had spotted Edith hidden in a clue involving 'the ditherer'. But she was on the wrong track for the crossword; the answer was six letters long, blank K blank L blank blank.

She had started doing crosswords with her father after his first cataract. 'Blank K blank L blank blank,' she would say after she had read him the clue, and he would usually get the answer with hardly a hesitation. Her memory nowadays was like a half-finished crossword. Parts of her life emerged in sharp focus from the surrounding blanks. But the blanks were never constant. Were her memory this clue, for instance, the K and L might be the blanks one day while the rest was clear – skills! Skills was the answer. She filled in the blanks.

Only three clues to go. At least she could still do crosswords but what other skills had she acquired during her long life?

Driving could be counted. She had learnt to drive at much the same time her father was losing his sight. Now she herself was banned from driving by her doctor. She had mixed feelings about this. For some years she had had to steel herself to venture forth in today's traffic; everyone drove so fast and aggressively; parking was a nightmare; she loathed the constriction of a safety belt. It was a relief to be forbidden to take part in the screeching, racing, pushing scrum. On the other hand, it was a severe handicap to be carless where she lived. It was two miles to the nearest shop and she could no longer walk the distance. There was no bus. Before the ban she used to drive Edith to the shops once a week. Edith had returned by taxi because she always went to the hairdresser after shopping and Vi was not expected to wait. Now they shared a taxi both ways. This meant Vi had to wait while Edith had her hair done.

Sometimes this took ages. Edith's hair was permed and tinted. Vi often thought that Edith should walk home after the particularly lengthy sessions. This would really justify all those compliments heaped on Edith about being marvellous for her age.

Edith had had not only a career but also a husband and a son. The husband had been killed in the black-out in the Second World War: knocked down by a bus. The child, apparently, was an engineer in New Zealand. Edith had worked in a bank somewhere in the North. She had a carriage clock on her mantelpiece which had been presented to her on her retirement.

Violet was sure that Edith despised her for being a member of the privileged classes. 'Of course you've never had to work,' was a typical Edith remark. 'It's all right for some,' was another, prompted by such events as the arrival of Violet's window-cleaner or chimney-sweep. Edith did everything herself. Violet thought that money had nothing to do with this difference in their ways of running their respective homes. She suspected that Edith was no worse off than she was herself. In fact she had moments when she thought Edith might be far better off. In the queue at the post office Edith seemed to take longer to count her benefit payments than Violet did. There were sometimes money orders from New Zealand to be cashed. There was no doubt a pension from the bank. Whereas she considered herself to be in straightened circumstances; almost a case for the Distressed Gentlefolk's Association, a charity for which she had canvassed in the past. Violet thought that the fact that she employed workmen while Edith did not was due to a difference in priorities, not incomes. Unlike Edith, she never spent money on her hair. She never bought nail polish or make-up or stockings that would ladder. She did not have a colour television and a video recorder. She had no washing machine. She never had new curtains or carpets or bedlinen or saucepans. The only gadget in her kitchen was an electric whisk. Edith was always buying expensive kitchen equipment: mixer–blenders, sandwich-makers, machines for making coffee, opening tins, slicing beans, disposing of rubbish. Recently she had bought a microwave oven. As though she had not all the time in the world to wait for things to cook!

Violet enjoyed cooking. Nanny Burton had taught her in the early 1940s, when the house was requisitioned and the two of them moved into the gardener's cottage where there was no room for any living-in staff. How Nanny Burton knew about cooking was a mystery because she had never had to prepare anything more elaborate than the early-morning tea trays with their plates of thinly sliced, crumbling, brown bread and butter. All she would offer by way of explanation was 'Cook told me' or 'Cook did it'. Nanny Burton taught Vi about keeping hens and growing vegetables too. At one point they even kept geese, and Vi could recall the sight of Nanny Burton, a frail little woman in high, buttoned boots, hanging a goose by its feet to the washing-line so that she could break its neck with a hefty swing of a broom handle.

'Surely Cook never did *that*?' asked Vi, feeling queasy. The answer was that was how Nanny Burton's father did it. This must have been one of the very few occasions when Nanny Burton ever mentioned her own family. Most of the time it was unthinkable that she had ever been a child herself or had relations of her own. Nanny was part of the family in much the same way as the house was part of the family. Now the house had become a convalescent home full of unknown people; and Nanny Burton was growing ill and old. Even then, Violet never thought to discover if there were any relations to notify. When Nanny died and Vi was asked to look through her private papers for the name of next-of-kin, it was a shock to discover that Nanny Burton was called Matilda Munroe. Violet learnt that the name Burton had come from the family which Nanny had nannied before she joined the Sharpes. In a box of letters there were photographs of babies and children, and most of them were not Sharpes but Burtons. Violet, aged forty-three, felt sick with jealousy.

Betty had been jealous too, but her jealousy sprang from the fact that Nanny Burton had left all her money to Vi. There had been no mention of Betty in the will. The sum involved was very small. Violet told Betty the exact figure and reminded her that it was she who had looked after Nanny for years. Betty replied that she would have done just the same had she not been abroad. For years afterwards Betty made sly allusions to the legacy in ways that made it sound substantial.

Even as a child Betty had thought that Vi was better off than she was herself. When she married her soldier, Arthur Drummond, and her parents gave them part of the garden on which to build a house, she had considered that the sum given to Vi as a fair equivalent in cash was not equivalent at all. It was far more generous. 'Of course, *we* haven't the money to build even a shed on it yet,' she would say, and her tone of voice would imply that Vi could build a mansion should she so desire. And when they were stationed in India she wrote, '*We* can't afford to come home on leave. *You* must visit us.' This was in 1927, soon after Father's death. Betty obviously had no idea how much nursing Mother needed.

Violet did go to India the following year. Mother had died in the meantime.

'At long last, we'll be able to build something for ourselves,' said Betty. 'We can sell the big house and the rest of the garden.'

Hadn't she read the will? Violet had been left the house and remaining garden, Betty the majority of the capital invested in stocks and shares.

'We?' she queried.

'Well, you won't want to go on living in that enormous place all on your own.'

'It's not really very big and I'm not on my own.'

Betty looked startled.

Vi continued, 'There's Nanny Burton and Cook. Elsie is still with us, though she's riddled with rheumatism. We have a daily coming in, and there's Sam in the garden.'

'Oh, you gave me quite a fright for a moment. I thought you must have gone and married that Irish friend of yours!'

Violet was taken aback. What on earth had made Betty entertain, however briefly, the idea that she might marry Patrick? What had Mother been saying in her letters? And why would her marriage, if ever such a thing occurred which seemed more and more unlikely – she was nearing thirty, for heaven's sake! – why would it give her sister 'quite a fright'?

'I don't want to sell the house. I like living there. I don't want to live anywhere else.' She spoke firmly.

Later, Arthur was called in on the side of reason. Unlike Betty, he had fully understood that the house and remaining garden belonged to Vi and if she sold it she would have the proceeds. 'That house must cost a fortune to run,' he pointed out. 'It's no surprise to me that your parents had eaten into their capital so much. You will never be able to afford it on the income from your share. The only course open to you, Violet, is to sell up.'

'No,' said Violet. 'I am going to take in paying guests.' She had just thought of this.

'*Paying guests!*' shrieked Arthur and Betty in unison.

After this, even more cocktail, tennis and bridge parties were arranged. 'Part of the fishing fleet?' she had overheard on the passage out. Now Violet understood what this meant. Arthur and Betty had obviously decided that it was imperative to find Violet a husband.

'Do you remember your grandmother at all?'

Stephen was startled by this abrupt question. He had been telling Aunty Vi about his plans for building a bike while they waited for their food to arrive. It was their seventh evening meal in the same restaurant. Each evening the waiters were more friendly and the meals less expensive.

'Yeah, a bit. We used to stay with them in London in the Christmas holidays and they took us to the theatre.' He remembered the room in the attic where he had slept surrounded by his father's childhood. Granny Winfield had kept the room in a fit state for the return of her son; as though at any moment he would ask for his skates or meccano set.

'No, not Granny Winfield,' said Aunty Vi. 'I mean Granny Drummond. My sister.'

Stephen looked at Vi as though seeing her for the first time. Of course he had known that she was Mum's aunt, but had he ever registered the fact that she was Granny Drummond's sister? The thought that Granny and Vi had once been little girls, sisters playing in the same house, was extraordinary. It gave him the same sort of feeling as he had when he had slept in his father's room and tried to imagine his father as a boy.

'Do you have any memories of her?' prompted Vi. 'How old were you when she died?'

Stephen searched for pictures from the past. The Mitchells lived next door in what had been his grandparents' house. The gate in the fence had been replaced by another lapwood panel and more bushes planted to fill the gap in the line. He could remember running after Vicky and Claire to visit his grandmother. Slipping through the gate had made him feel like a rabbit disappearing down a burrow. They had done it secretly. Perhaps Mum had not wanted them to visit Granny too often because she gave them sweets. On a shelf below the kitchen hatch there was a red tin with women in bonnets dancing on the lid. The tin was full of sweets of every kind. Sometimes she gave them hot chocolate and biscuits. Her hands had brown spots on the backs. She smelt like something that had been kept in a drawer too long; a faded lavender, faintly musty smell. Now he came to think of it, there was a vaguely similar smell about his great-aunt. He could not recall his grandmother's face at all. Had she looked like Aunty Vi? 'I do remember her a bit,' he said. 'Did you use to look alike?'

'Did you use to! Really! Never mind. When we were small, we were often dressed alike. But I don't think we looked alike. Betty took after Mother. She was pretty. She had beautiful auburn hair. I was more like Father. Rather plain!'

Stephen looked at his great-aunt's face, testing the words 'pretty' and 'plain'. Had people thought Aunty Vi too plain to marry? He tried to imagine the skin without the puckered lines and her chin without the two lizard-like lines of sinewy flesh that led to the collar of her blue blouse. Her nose would always have been a little beaked. She was watching him with an amused expression in her eyes and he looked down at the bread basket in front of him.

'You're not plain,' he said. He wanted to say something more. A jumble of thoughts was going through his mind – about girls' looks – about how the words 'plain' and 'pretty' didn't come into it – about how it was the people inside who counted because that showed in the expression – and why had Aunty Vi never married?

But she was now talking about a place called Rawalpindi where she had stayed with Betty. Stephen was lost for a moment until there was mention of Major Drummond. Betty was the name of his grandmother, of course. His grandfather would have been a major at the time. Stephen remembered him being referred to as 'Brig'.

He ate the moussaka that had arrived in front of him while Aunty Vi rambled on. He was not interested in stories about long train rides to Kashmir and how his great-aunt had shocked people at a tea party by talking in Hindustani with a servant. He wanted to hear about the days when his grandparents lived next door. There was something very comforting and intriguing about being taken back and linked to his childhood after six months on his own in a foreign land.

'Didn't we use to play charades or something at Granny's

house at Christmas?' he prompted at a suitable pause. Aunty Vi must have been with them on these occasions. It was only quite recently that she had stopped coming to them for Christmas.

'Oh, I left before Christmas. I was only there three months. They had hoped I would stay longer but really the attentions of this dreadful man were becoming too much altogether . . . I cannot imagine why Betty thought I might fall for him. He was such a drip!'

'No. At Granny's house in England.'

'What about it, dear?'

'Charades, games and things, at Christmas-time.'

'Oh yes.' Aunty Vi laid down her fork and pushed aside her plate.

'Have you finished that?' asked Stephen.

His great-aunt handed him her half-eaten moussaka without comment. His regular finishing of her meals had become accepted.

'Yes, we had wonderful dressing-up clothes, didn't we? That oak coffer in my bedroom used to be full of the most gorgeous garments. I would have kept them but Betty was such a rigorous thrower-away of things. I suppose it was being in the Army. Always on the move.'

'Did I dress up? I don't remember.'

Aunty Vi looked at him with a puzzled expression. 'Ah. Stephen.' She lapsed into silence.

'At Granny's house,' he tried again.

'Really, I don't remember very well these days, dear. You must forgive me.'

Stephen mentally drew a big, fat exclamation mark in a cartoon bubble over the table. Aunty Vi had spent the last half-hour remembering.

'May I suggest,' she said as they walked slowly back to the hotel, 'that you give the van a good tidy-up tomorrow morning while I'm at the bank. You never know, the money may be through and we'll be able to leave.'

She had made this suggestion every day since the drive

from the hospital. This time he agreed to do it with conviction in his voice. Aunty Vi had washed various handfuls of clothes he had brought in from the van, and now 'tidying-up' didn't seem such a monstrous task. Besides, by agreeing, he smoothed the path for the next step: his regular evening request for cash. Unlike the half-finished plates of food, his need for cash had not been accepted without comment. But she always handed something over in the end, even if it was barely enough for a drink and a packet of fags. She didn't smoke herself and she wasn't drinking. She obviously found it hard to imagine that he might need the occasional drink and a smoke. She always seemed surprised that he didn't want to go to sleep at half-past nine. 'These late nights!' she would exclaim. 'No wonder you can never wake up in the morning.'

What on earth did she think there was to wake up for? He could go for a walk, visit the museum, swim in the lake. These suggestions of hers were pathetic. She might as well suggest he made a macramé plant-pot hanger. Only the nights in this one-eyed town were halfway bearable. And without the boost of alcohol and the occasional smoke, it was far more likely that he would have jumped in the lake than swum in it.

Stephen made his way down to the lake to see if the students were still around. They had gone. He sat down in the deserted café and brooded over a brandy. He had been looking forward to the journey home. Now it looked as though he would be stuck in Greece with Aunty Vi for ever. The money wouldn't arrive. They'd be turned back at the border. The van would break down. He hadn't got a girlfriend. There was nothing waiting for him at home. He'd be back in the same old rut hassling to get supplementary benefit. Life was a shit-hole. He couldn't even get in the van and drive back to find Jake. He had no money, no petrol. He was stuck with Aunty Vi.

By midday on Friday 5th September, Stephen and Violet had started on their journey home. The blue van climbed the tawny hills out of Petropolis trailing swirls of dust and exhaust fumes over the roadside thistles.

'Are you sure we've got everything? Done everything?' Violet felt anxious. It had been rather a rush in the end.

'Petrol, water, tyres,' said Stephen. 'Luggage.'

'Passports. Paid hospital. Paid hotel. Bought picnic. We'll stop at the first nice place, shall we?'

'Oh no, let's get to Igoumenitsa. It's only an hour or so from here.' He could still taste the sweetness of the sticky cakes he had bought with the change from the garage.

'An hour! But I'm really rather peckish. Breakfast seems ages ago.'

'Okay then. Look out for a place.' The engine was missing on the hills. He hoped Aunty Vi hadn't noticed. He didn't want her getting into a flap. It was probably only a bit of dirt in the carburettor. Or water in the petrol. As soon as they reached the crest of the next hill, he would step on the gas and clear it.

'Oh, Stephen!' Aunty Vi's hand was on the door. 'Must you drive so fast? I don't feel at all safe sitting so high up.'

'We're only doing fifty-five. It just seems fast.' He pointed at the needle on the speedometer. It was jiggling as usual between fifty and eighty miles per hour. 'Bessie can't go much above seventy anyway,' he added as he saw Vi peering at the dial just as the needle glanced off eighty.

'Bessie! Why Bessie? A wee bit slower, there's a dear.'

'Just a name. I like saying it.'

'I had a bike I called James,' said Aunty Vi.

Stephen thought he should be polite about this. 'Oh yeah?' he said. Fancy giving a bicycle a name.

'It was a BSA Bantam. Green. I loved it.'

It couldn't be true! Aunty Vi on a BSA! 'When was this?'

'During the war. I joined the WVS in the war and drove for the Ministry of Food occasionally. Someone I met had a Bantam and sold it to me. I used to ride over to visit Betty whenever I could get petrol. Black market, of course!'

'Black market?'

'I used to give the girls rides on the back up and down the drive.'

'What girls?'

'Elizabeth and Diana.'

'What? Mum?'

'Yes, of course. Your mother and aunt. They used to be dressed alike. Oh heavens, the morning-room curtains! I remember those dresses so well. Your mother burst into tears. She was seven. I gave her a five-pound piece to cheer her up.'

'A five-pound piece?' He pulled in to the side of the road to let a lorry pass. All this startling information had made him drive much slower. 'But that's what Mum sold to give me this van! It must have been the same one. It was 1884 or something.'

'Then it probably was the same one. My great-aunt Beatrice gave it to me when I was seven. She gave me such a lecture too. I was terrified. She had an ear trumpet which we had to shout into. Look, there's a place. Shall we stop here?'

Stephen braked and just managed to turn down the track Violet was pointing at. It led to a riverbed.

'I shall need my binoculars here,' said Aunty Vi when

they had settled themselves on a rock with their picnic. 'Be a dear and find them for me. I think I tucked them under the seat. Or did I leave them in my suitcase? Or they could be in that little hold-all.'

'Yes, it's a black-headed bunting,' she told him with satisfaction when he eventually returned with the binoculars. 'Would you like to look? It's in that tamarisk.'

Stephen took the binoculars and fiddled with the focus as he aimed them in the direction of the bush. He was interested in the glasses, not the bird. They were unlike any he had seen before. They, and their battered leather case, were probably as old as Aunty Vi.

'It's gone,' she pointed out. 'It's over there now. Oh, and there's a crested lark. This is wonderful. And the butterflies! How father would have loved this. The binoculars were his, you know.'

As Stephen handed the binoculars back, he suddenly wanted to possess them. It wasn't that they were particularly good. It was more to do with – what was it exactly? History, personal history. Aunty Vi was linking him to a past that belonged to him as much as it did to her. Vi's father, her great-aunt Beatrice, the two little girls one of whom was his mother – he was part of them, they were part of him. Vi herself, sitting on her rock chanting with excitement the names of birds, had become part of him. She had been simply Aunty Vi, an object with a name, like his van. He could no longer think of her in this way. She had become a person with whom he was concerned, someone he wanted to get to know.

'Tell me about your bike,' he said.

Beyond the fact that it was an olive-greeny colour, Vi knew nothing about her bike. She couldn't answer any of his questions. But she told him other things that he found interesting. There had been no signposts in the war. Several times she had got lost driving between the place where she had been living with a friend called Ivy and his grandmother's house. His grandmother's house was built in the garden of the old house where she had grown up.

'Which house?' He pictured his home, the Mitchells' house which had belonged to his grandparents, and the surrounding houses. But for an old cottage called The Lodge where he had imagined Hansel and Gretel lived, all the houses were modern. They were built of red-brick and had integral garages. The curving roads that linked them were called Cedar Close, Acacia Avenue and The Oaks. As he searched in his mind along these roads he could see no sign of a house old enough.

'It was pulled down after the war. Your mother must remember it. Hasn't she told you about it?'

'I knew that our house was built in Granny's garden. But I don't remember being told about another house. Where was it exactly?'

'It's almost impossible to describe, the place is unrecognizable with all those new estates. Your house is where the tennis court used to be. From there you could go up some steps, across another lawn, up some more steps to a gravel terrace and there was the house. One day I'll show you a photograph.'

Stephen was imagining something out of a kind of antiquated English Dallas. 'Did it have all that land? It must have been huge.'

'Oh no, not at all. It was a perfectly ordinary sort of house for our sort of people in those days.'

Vi lapsed into silence.

What were 'our sort of people'? Stephen wondered. Was he an our sort of person? In the eyes of his friends, his parents were well off. He knew they could have afforded to send him away to school but hadn't done this on the grounds of what they called their principles. Stephen found his parents' attitudes puzzling. It didn't seem to have anything to do with money. His friends' attitudes had everything to do with money.

'Were your parents rich?' he asked. 'What did your father do?'

'He didn't have to work, he had a private income.'

Aunty Vi must have a private income too. Stephen wished he had lived in those days.

'But he was always doing things,' she went on. 'He used to experiment with photography. He had a dark room. He used to collect butterflies and he was rather a good painter. He painted landscapes and butterflies and birds. He read a lot and wrote letters to *The Times*. He also used to translate Latin and Greek poetry, but simply for his own pleasure. He never published any of his translations though I'm sure he could have done. People thought they were very clever. Amazing to think of it these days, isn't it? People were educated for leisure. Now they are educated for work that doesn't exist.'

What did she mean by this? He had noticed her habit of issuing broadly sweeping statements from a narrow outlook and limited experience. He wondered how he could challenge her on this but she was continuing.

'What are *you* going to do, Stephen?'

Well, at least it had taken a week for her to ask this question. 'Sign on,' he said. He screwed their picnic's paper bags into a ball which he tossed into the river. 'Shouldn't we hit the road?' He didn't want the conversation to take this turn.

Violet got to her feet with difficulty and went to the water's edge. She managed to hook the bag with her stick and pull it out of the water. She bent down, picked it up and squeezed the water out of it. She then put it in the pocket of her dress. 'Have you noticed,' she asked, 'that I'm wearing a shoe on my foot today? That's progress, isn't it?'

As they walked back to the van, Violet noticed for the first time the decoration on the back doors. 'My goodness, what is that?' she asked.

'My hands,' said Stephen. 'I think I used the wrong kind of paint.' He had taken prints of his hands, enlarged them and painted an approximation of the result on the rear of the van, a giant red hand with black lines on each door.

Since then some of the paint had chipped and a layer of dust obscured the lower half.

Violet looked more closely and held her hand, fingers outstretched, an inch or two from one of the doors. 'Were you pushing the van?' she asked.

Could she really think his hands were that big? 'Blown up,' he said.

'The van blew up?'

'Never mind,' he said with a smile. It was a waste of time trying to explain. Instead he herded her towards the passenger door.

'Well, I hope it doesn't happen again. I won't be able to push,' she said as he hoisted her into the seat.

He went round to his door and opened it. 'Nothing wrong with Bess,' he said climbing in. 'She goes like a bomb. Downhill with the wind behind her.'

'So I notice,' said Vi. 'Now have we got everything?'

'Your binoculars?'

She had left them on the rock.

'I'd hate to lose these,' she said, clasping the binoculars on her lap when they were once more on their way. After a moment she went on. 'It's a strange thing about objects. I mean, things that have belonged to someone you loved. Things that they have used and loved. It's as though something of the people you loved lingers in their possessions. Or do you think it's simply that their possessions make us think of them?'

Stephen had no remark to offer. This was outside his experience. No one he knew had ever died. No, not true. His grandparents. But he could hardly remember any of them.

'Do you believe in an afterlife, Stephen?' asked Violet in a while. 'It would be interesting to know what the young think.'

'What? When you die, you mean? What happens?'

'Yes.'

'Nothing. I don't believe in God and all that –' He restrained himself from saying 'crap'. 'I think death is death, the end, finito. Nothing else.'

Nuffin! Violet was beginning to like the way Stephen spoke. Perhaps by the time they got home, she'd be saying nuffin and sumfin. 'There's nuffin, nuffin, nuffin like a Puffin,' she sang.

Stephen glanced at her, mystified.

'That was a, what do they call it, an advertising song. Jingle, that's it. Selling Puffin books. Not so long ago.'

What was she on about?

'I think I'll just close my eyes now,' she said.

She was asleep! And a moment ago she'd just begun an interesting conversation about death. He would make sure he never grew old. The bomb would see to that in any case.

Violet struggled feebly to sit more upright. Slumped in such an awkward position it was hard to focus the binoculars, and her view of the gardener's cottage was hazy. One thing she could see clearly was the small black gate on which The Lodge was painted in white. She knew she had to warn the two people inside. What the danger was and who the people were, she was not sure. One was Nanny Burton but a Nanny Burton that looked and spoke like a young Ivy. The other might be herself? Yes, she was inside the cottage now, boarding up the windows. Ivy was climbing up the stairs on her hands and knees to get a view from the upstairs windows. Was the cottage about to be demolished? There were people outside, swarming in from the direction of the big house. They were wounded. They wore bandages and limped, some leaning on their sticks, some brandishing them. There was shouting and screaming and smoke. She knew she ought not to stay inside the cottage. She should try and reach the big house and save the family. The awful thing was that the wounded people were coming from the big house. How could she be sure which were the wounded attackers and which were the family? They were mixed up. She was limping along a suburban road called The Oaks. A man was washing his car. She was pleading with him to tell her something but he kept saying, 'There's no one here.' He was right. The road was empty. She went on walking. The road became very steep and Ivy was helping her up the stairs. 'It's the Shah of Balham,' said Ivy who was wearing gypsy earrings and a coin-fringed headscarf. Ivy laughed and laughed.

'What did you say?' asked Violet.

'Igoumenitsa,' said Stephen. 'We're here. I'm going to stop at that travel agent's.'

'What I long for, more than anything in the world, is a cup of tea,' said Violet. 'From a teapot.'

'I've got a teapot,' said Stephen. 'If we can buy some decent tea, we could brew up.' He swung the van across the road and pulled up outside the travel agent's office. The large plate-glass windows were covered with posters advertising ferry lines. CHEAPEST! FASTEST! LOOK HERE! Inside, a single desk was visible and at the desk a man slept, his head on his arms. 'I hope it's open. It's siesta time.'

Violet watched Stephen approach the door. It was shut and obviously locked. He knocked. The man at the desk slept on. Stephen then banged on the window at a point opposite the desk. There was no reaction. He bent and picked up a small pebble.

'Stephen! Don't!' Vi had visions of paying an enormous bill for a smashed plate-glass window. She seized her stick from the floor and banged the half-open driver's window. 'Don't, Stephen!'

The stick's noise attracted his attention and he came across to the van. 'It's shut,' he said, bending down to look in.

'You're not going to throw that stone at the window, are you?'

'It's not a stone. It's money.' He handed her a silver coin. 'A hundred lira!'

Violet looked down at the coin in her hand. 'We can't keep this. Give it to the man in the office. Someone will be missing it.'

But Stephen was no longer there. The office door had been opened and he was being ushered to a chair by the desk.

Violet wondered if she had the energy to get out of the van and join him in the office. She decided there was no need for this. Stephen could find out about ferries perfectly well on his own. She heard herself sigh with relief. It was nice to have someone to deal with things. She put the coin on the driver's seat.

The Shah of Balham! She laughed. Was that what she had been dreaming about? It had been a frightening dream; she could recall the sensation of terror. The seance had been frightening as well as funny. It hadn't really been a seance. More a game. Ivy had taken her to a party.

It was quite unlike any party she had ever been to before.

She was lent a dress by Ivy, who considered Vi hopelessly old-fashioned. Stockings, too. Her own were too coarse to be revealed to the world by the shortness of the dress. She should have let Ivy cut her hair off before the party rather than after it. But she hadn't been quite brave enough for this. As it was, Ivy brushed it till it hung straight and long behind her shoulders and then tied it cleverly in a loop with a sequined band.

They went by tube to Putney. This was a frightening adventure in itself. Vi kept her gloved hand securely tucked into the warm crook of Ivy's arm. The hot rush of wind on the platform before the train emerged from the tunnel would have lifted their skirts had not Ivy warned her. The roar of the approaching train seemed to go right through her. Once on the rackety, clattering monster, Ivy talked all the time. Vi regretted the loudness of Ivy's voice; it attracted attention. But she was greedy for its information. The more she learnt, the more she wondered why Ivy could be bothered with someone as ill-informed and dull as herself. She would never learn to talk of all these '-isms' so blithely: socialism, post-impressionism, Fabianism, feminism, journalism. This last was one to which she could have given a definition if challenged. But she hoped she would not be challenged. She was beginning to wish she had stayed at home.

It was a long walk from the tube to the house where the party was being held. They threaded their way, left then right, left then right, through a grid of roads lined with blossoming cherries. Lights were coming on in ground-floor windows.

'What do all these people *do*? Where do they all work?' Violet could understand the crowds and bustle of London but the sight of so many homes so far from the centre was a surprise. They had left behind the workmen's terraces of the High Street area and were now passing houses of a kind she had not seen before. Some stood alone in little gardens. Others were divided into two; but the division was not an afterthought. It had been planned. Each half had its gable, its chimneys, its matching windows, front door and porch.

'They work in London, of course. In shops and offices, I daresay.'

At home she had never questioned what people did. It was all obvious. There was the town and the townspeople; there was the countryside and the country people; there were the people her parents knew. She could not imagine what other sort of people there could be.

'Will they be at the party?' asked Vi. She knew she sounded foolish as soon as she had spoken. 'I mean – those sort of people?'

Ivy hugged her. 'You really are –' she began with a laugh. Then she went on, 'I've no idea who'll be there. Gerhard and Lettice, the ones giving the party, are, well, it's almost impossible to explain. Let's say they're economists. Gerhard is German. He's over here doing research. He met Lettice at London University. She's actually an anthropologist.'

Vi definitely wished she had stayed at home.

'Anthony will be there. Anthony Lejeune? You don't know his name? But you read *The Times*, I know.'

'Is he a journalist?'

'I want you two to meet. I think you'll get on.'

Germans! Anthropologists! Journalists!

Ivy laughed again. 'Oh Vi, you can't be nervous. All you have to do is what you are so good at doing. Listen with those big blue eyes of yours.' Ivy took her hand and pulled her along the pavement. Vi had almost come to a halt. 'And make those occasionally pithy comments of yours,' she added.

This was a view of herself Vi had never entertained. But the idea that Ivy thought her capable of 'pithy comments' gave her courage to enter the party and, although there were stretches of time when she pressed herself into a corner unattended, she managed to survive. There were people in each of the three downstairs rooms. There were people sitting on the stairs. By the sound of it, there were even people upstairs, but Vi didn't venture that far. She did meet the journalist but she didn't understand why Ivy had thought they would get on. He had a dreadful stammer and, as Vi had little idea what he was talking about when he could get the words out, there were long tracts of silence when he couldn't. She was relieved when eventually he said he had to get home. There were only six or seven people left by this time. Ivy showed no signs of wishing to go. She, it turned out, had been waiting for this moment to get down to what she described as the main point of the evening. Lettice stoked the fire. Gerhard placed a low table, painted black with a star-burst in red and gold, in the centre of the room. Ivy threw cushions on the floor around the table. Someone called Gerald was sent to find a clean glass in the kitchen. Earlier in the evening she had been introduced to him. He was a painter so Violet had told him about her father's watercolours. He had not appeared very interested in this information. A girl called Marie with golden hair like a Botticelli angel sat down on a cushion and patted the one beside her for Violet; but a man with immensely long legs sat down on it first. It was like watching a crane-fly land.

There was a burst of laughter. Violet had said this aloud.

'Will you sit next to a crane-fly?' the man asked. He said his name was Philip. 'We need pencil and paper, don't we. Lettice! Paper!' He turned to Vi. 'Have you ever played this silly game before?'

'What is it? Consequences? Heads, bodies and legs?'

There was more laughter. After this, everything Violet said amused the company. She was not sure whether the laughter was with her or at her but she had drunk enough wine not to mind.

Philip and Marie were arranging the letters of the alphabet in a circle on the table. The letters came from a game of Lexicon. The box lay open beside Violet and she strained to read the rules printed on the inside of the lid. This must be a version of the game she had not come across. Gerald returned with a glass which Gerhard set upside-down in the centre of the table's star pattern. There was some discussion about the darkness of the room. Would one candle give enough light? Would two destroy the atmosphere? Where should the candle or candles be placed? Could they somehow drape Marie's red scarf over a lamp for a suitably subdued glow? Marie said no, they couldn't. Eventually the lighting arrangements were setttled. Lettice lit one candle of a three-branched candlestick and placed it on a tall plant table, having banished its previous occupant, a trailing fern, to the hall.

'Pencil and paper,' Philip reminded Lettice.

'But we've got the letters.'

'For the messages. We'll want to write them down as they're spelt out.'

Ivy leant across the table and touched Violet's arm. 'It's not frightening, truly.'

Violet was bewildered, not frightened. 'Are we going to write messages?' she asked.

'Certainly not!' barked Gerhard. 'There is to be no pushing. Anyone who cheats . . .' He paused, searching for a suitable punishment. 'Anyone who cheats goes down to the cellar for more coal.'

This produced an outcry.

'We never push,' said Ivy. 'Do we, Lettice?'

'I'm sure Philip pushed last time. Remember? It spelt out Angel and the next word was Mons.'

'No it wasn't,' said Philip. 'It was angry mouse. And I didn't push!'

'Angry mouse indeed!'

Gerhard clapped his hands. 'Now. We do not want to start that argument again. Fingers on!'

Violet watched the others and then tentatively touched the glass with the tip of her index finger in the same way.

'Now concentrate!'

For a moment there was silence. Everyone's head was bent towards the glass and their eyes were fixed on the circle of fingers.

'I've got cramp,' whispered Ivy.

'Shush.'

'I have got awful cramp. I shall have to move.'

'Oh, Ivy!'

Ivy rearranged herself on her cushion.

'Now concentrate,' said Gerhard once more.

The candle sputtered in its candlestick and threw glancing shadows on the table. On the mantelpiece a wooden-cased clock ticked throatily. The group's breathing patterns became audible. Marie began giggling.

'Marie!' They all scolded her.

'I'm sorry. It's just that. I felt. A sneeze.' She sneezed.

'For heaven's sake, settle down, all of you. We'll be here all night.' Gerhard sounded bad-tempered.

'Is anyone there?' asked Philip in a cheery manner. They all laughed.

'Philip! Do be serious.' Lettice was beginning to sound cross too.

'Is anybody there? said the traveller, knocking on the old inn door.'

'Philip! You'll be in the coal cellar.'

'Let Gerhard do the talking. It's best if only one of us asks.'

'I am not going to start until everyone is absolutely silent and –' Gerhard interrupted himself with a sneeze that shattered the circle. They all fell back laughing. It was some time before he regained control of them.

When he had achieved a long-enough silence, he began talking in a low voice as though to himself. 'We are waiting,' he said. 'We are ready to be in touch. We are waiting. We would like a message. Has anyone a message for us?' After a moment, he talked again. 'We are ready for a message. Is there anyone there with a message?'

The way he spoke accentuated the darkness and silence of the room. Violet felt her skin prickle. She had realized what was happening. She thought of Tom.

'Is there anyone there with a message for us?' Gerhard's voice was quickening and under her finger Violet felt the glass shiver.

The circle of heads, without a movement, seemed to draw closer and more intent.

The glass began a journey across the table. It slid towards the letter A and then slowly moved sideways to the letter F. There it stood for a moment.

'A , F,' whispered Ivy.

'Not A, it didn't stop there.'

'Shush, it's started again.'

The glass shot fast across the table and nudged the X.

'A, F, X?'

'A fox? Are you a fox?'

'Don't be absurd, Gerhard. How can a fox send messages?'

'Like Philip's angry mouse!'

'Who's writing the letters down? Marie? You write them down.'

'I can't write with my left hand.'

'Shush.'

The glass returned to A, then on to G. It seemed to hesitate at M and then returned to the centre of the table.

'Is that your name?' asked Gerhard. The glass made a

short sideways movement. 'That's no. It said no. Is that a place?'

'Ask if it has a message for someone here.'

'Wait. It's just saying yes, but I don't know what to.'

Gerald had written down the letters. 'F, X, A, G, M. Doesn't make sense. Start again, Gerhard.'

Gerhard called for silence. 'Tell us your name,' he said.

Under Violet's finger the glass felt lifeless. It was just an object. She closed her eyes and imagined being blind. When you touch a tree, you can feel it is a live thing. She remembered a pair of secateurs snipping the stem of a rose. Under her finger, the glass trembled. Her eyes shot open.

The glass moved straight towards her. The letters nearest her went from R on her right to W on her left.

'That was T,' said someone.

'No, it's going on . . .'

'V.'

'No, W.'

The glass moved to the opposite side of the table.

'I.'

'No, H.'

It began circling back and wavered from O to M and then back to O. Vi removed her finger from the glass.

'I think that was W, H, O. It wants to know who we want to speak to.'

'It was T, I, M. Who knows a Tim?'

'Or a Tom?'

Violet was trembling. 'My brother was called Tom,' she said. She had thought the glass had spelt out not Tom but the first three letters of her own name. She was not at all sure she wanted to continue with this.

'It was Tom then!' cried Marie excitedly. 'Let's ask it!'

Philip had noticed Violet's dismay. 'Perhaps you'd rather not,' he said quietly.

Violet did not know. This had been an amusing game but now . . . could it be possible that Tom was there, trying to speak to her through a glass on a table at a party? She did not want to stop but she was frightened to continue. There was something malevolent about the atmosphere, something which could not have anything to do with Tom. She told herself that someone in the group must be pushing the glass, someone who wanted to scare her. Perhaps it was Gerhard or Gerald.

'Oh no, let's carry on,' she said putting her finger back on the glass. She would not think of Tom or of anything at all. This was simply a party game.

The glass was returned to the centre of the table and Gerhard began his questions once more. 'Have you a message for us?'

The glass moved from letter to letter, N, U, T, S.

They laughed.

'Who are you?' asked Gerhard.

Gerald wrote down the letters of the answer with his left hand: T, H, E, S, H, A, H, O, F, B, A, L, H, A, M.

Stephen was at the window of the van.

'Any luck?' she asked.

'Bit of a problem,' he said. 'They can get us a ferry the day after tomorrow. It leaves at six on Sunday evening and takes twelve hours. But another agent might get us on one tomorrow. Trouble is, he says, if we don't book at once we might not get on the Sunday ferry. What should we do?'

'How far away are the other agents?'

'They're right in the town. Another mile or so.'

The thought of waiting until Sunday evening was not attractive. 'Shall we risk it?' suggested Vi. 'We can be back here in half an hour if we don't have luck elsewhere.'

As it turned out, it was an hour before they returned. Stephen had tried every other agent and none could offer them tickets for a ferry sooner than Monday. An Italian camping van was now parked outside the office. Stephen hurried in as the Italian party came out. Violet's heart sank. She should not have suggested they try elsewhere.

She joined Stephen in the office.

'Monday at six in the morning,' he told her. 'I've booked it.'

'I am sorry. That was my fault,' she said.

'No it wasn't. I thought it was worth trying, too.'

'No, I should have known better. One must take one's opportunities when they arise. How stupid of me.'

'Forget it, it's only another night after all.'

'Yes, and that means three nights here. And your parents waiting! We must ring them tonight and tell them about the delays.' She sat down on a chair by the desk and took her wallet from her handbag. 'Now, how much is this going to cost?' She sounded tired and despairing.

While Vi dealt with the tickets Stephen went out to the van. He had decided that he would make a pot of tea; that would cheer her up. He set the kettle to boil on the gas ring and rubbed dust off two mugs wondering meanwhile how old his great-aunt could be. His grandmother had died when he was very young and Vi was her sister. Could he ask Vi her age? His mother never minded telling people she was forty-seven – or was she forty-eight now? But some women were cagey about their age, he knew. Maybe he could look at Vi's passport. Whatever age she was, she was pretty good for it, he thought; coming out here on holiday, putting up with the difficulties, not complaining about her leg, though that was obviously better. He wondered if she would manage to climb into the back of the van. Then they could drink their tea sitting on the mattress-covered bench. He could put Vi's luggage on the floor. After his tidying-up session there was room for this. But where had he put the teapot? And the tin of tea?

By the time Vi returned to the van he had found both. 'In the back!' he called as she passed the driver's window. 'I've made a pot of tea!'

'Tea, did you say?' she asked, appearing at the open rear door. 'What a treat – but I'll never climb up there,' she said.

Stephen got out. 'I'll lift you in,' he said. He clasped her around her waist. 'Duck your head,' he said.

'Stephen! Don't! Wait!' she cried, but he had picked her up. She began laughing helplessly.

'Bend your knees,' he instructed.

The next moment he had swung her into the van and climbed in after her.

'Sit yourself down, then I can pull out the table.'

The table was a piece of hardboard hinged below the sink.

'If you rest your leg on your hold-all . . .'

She did as she was told.

'There. Not too bad, is it?' He felt proud of his van. 'Now for the tea.' He put the pot and two mugs on the table. 'I had some of those little cartons of milk from the hotel . . .' He rummaged in the pocket of his jeans and produced four. 'There. Enough for two cups each.'

He sat down beside her.

'Shall I be mother?' asked Vi in a voice that mocked the expression.

'Go ahead.'

The tea was a murky yellow colour and leaves floated in it. 'I don't suppose you have a strainer, do you?' she asked.

'No. What me and Jake did sometimes was to pour it through a vest. That got rid of the leaves.'

'I expect they'll settle,' said Vi hastily. There was the smell of gas in the van. 'Is that thing turned off?' she asked pointing at the stove. 'Maybe you should open both the back doors.'

'Can't. All that stuff would fall out.'

It was extraordinarily hot in the van but Vi wouldn't complain. Stephen was obviously enjoying himself. She watched him roll a cigarette. 'My father had a cigarette-rolling machine,' she said, 'though he rarely smoked. It was silver, a beautiful thing.'

Stephen grunted. He lit his cigarette, which had a droop in the middle, and leant back. 'This is the life, eh. Everything you want. Independent.'

Vi, at the moment, found it hard to share his enthusiasm; she was feeling a little dizzy. She took a sip of tea. 'My goodness! What is this?'

'Isn't it any good?' he asked. 'It's camomile.'

'Camomile! It isn't tea at all!'

'It is. It's very good for you. Very good for settling the stomach. But it's been lying around a fair time.'

Vi pushed her mug away. 'I think perhaps I'll wait until we can find some proper tea,' she said.

Stephen sipped from his mug. There was nothing wrong with the tea. Old people get set in their ways, he thought; unwilling to try anything new.

'Was Granny Drummond much older than you?' he asked. This might be the clever way to discover her age.

Vi blinked. 'Two years,' she said. 'What on earth has that to do with tea?'

'Nothing,' he admitted. 'I was just wondering. Granny was much older than my friends' grandmothers.'

'Well, that would have been because she had children so late in life. There was a little boy. Jack. He was born in 1924 when Betty was, let me see, twenty-six. But he died of whooping cough. No innoculations in those days. Then there was a long gap. Diana was born in '36 and your mother in '38. Your grandmother was forty when your mother was born. We were quite worried at the time.'

Stephen was doing sums with difficulty. Then he realized the sums were easy. 'Then you're the same age as the century!' he said triumphantly.

'So that's why you asked,' said Vi with a smile. 'Yes, as old as the century. I don't feel that old. That is, my body certainly does but I myself . . . well, I'm about thirty or forty. No, it's not quite like that. More that I feel ageless. I am just trapped in an ageing body. I expect everyone feels the same.'

'I don't think I do,' said Stephen after a moment.

'But you're not old.'

'I do feel trapped though.' He relit his drooping cigarette. 'I wish I'd lived in the time of primitive man. That's what I wish.'

He embarked on a long description of the kind of life he

wished it was possible to live; hunting for food, sleeping in a cave, wearing animal skins, telling stories at night round a fire. 'Things would make sense,' he said. 'You'd know what you had to do.'

'Keep alive,' said Vi. 'Do you think that's our sole purpose? We just have to try to keep alive?'

'Yeah, and that's what's so bloody hard to do today.'

'Wasn't it hard then?'

'Mammoths and things you mean?' He pronounced it mammuffs. 'Right, so there were dangers. You might get killed by a bloody great mammoth. But it would make sense. You'd know why it was trying to kill you. Or if it was a rival tribe, you'd know why. They'd be after your hunting ground.'

'But aren't wars still fought for the same reason? Wouldn't you fight for your country if it was invaded? My two brothers were killed fighting for their country. One was twenty-one, the other twenty-two.'

'Like Vietnam. I saw this film. They were nineteen. Their own bloody fault. I wouldn't fight for any country – apart from meself. I'd fight for food but nowadays you have to fight the DHSS not mammoths.'

'What *do* you mean? They look after people who don't have work. People on unemployment benefit get well looked after. It's not like the old days when people literally starved . . . I remember seeing terrible sights in the Depression –'

'You don't know what it's like,' Stephen interrupted. 'I do. Before I left, I was getting fourteen quid a week supplementary. That was because they wouldn't give me unemployment benefit because I'd left my previous job for the wrong reason. I'd left my previous job because it was one of these schemes, digging old grunters' gardens and to get on that scheme you have to be unemployed for two months and they found out I'd had a job before that so they threw me off. And the job I'd had before that was only temporary and I'd gone away to live so that I could get on this scheme and the room I rented cost thirty-five quid a week and the scheme paid only forty-three, so I tried to get help from the rent office and that meant queuing and forms for weeks and it hadn't come through by the time I was chucked off the scheme so I had to come home. And that's when they said I would only get fourteen quid a week. So, okay, I was living at home and my parents were feeding me. But I don't want to live at home and have my parents feed me. I'm not a kid. I'm not mentally deficient or a cripple. I want to be independent. I don't mind hard work if I get paid for it. That's why I left. And that's why I don't want to go back.'

Violet slowly assimilated this confusing tale. Stephen obviously felt badly treated, but to her he sounded well cosseted, supported by both the state and his family. He had a van of his own – thanks, she remembered, to her great-aunt Beatrice. He had not starved. He had had work. He had been abroad enjoying himself for six months. He was spoilt. He expected too much. What he needed, she thought, was a spell in a Great War trench. She pulled herself up sharply. She would not wish this on anyone. And she herself had spent her life being cosseted. She had never worked. Even for the ten years of running the house for paying guests, she had done little but organize the household. Her years in the WVS could not be considered work, for she loved driving and was not paid for it. Really her life had been much as Stephen's promised to be. She glanced at him. He had buried his head on his arms on the table. She put a hand on his shoulder. 'You don't want to go back?' she asked.

He straightened up. 'No. There's nothing for me there.'

There was nothing for her there either. What had she to look forward to? The arrival of the post? Circulars, bank statements, bills; most of the friends who had written the occasional letter were dead. The arrival of Mrs Blatchett to do the housework? Mrs Blatchett was a bore. A trip with Edith by taxi to the town? She hated it. Christmas with the Winfields? That had stopped since she gave up driving.

Neither David nor Elizabeth ever thought of offering to drive over to collect her. Perhaps, after this trip, Stephen would think of it. She must not let herself sink into a depression especially as Stephen seemed to be sunk in one himself.

'Who knows what might not turn up?' she said brightly. 'In the meantime, shouldn't we go back into the town and find a hotel? We don't want to find all the rooms have been booked while we sat here drinking tea. And that's something we can do while we wait for Monday's ferry. We can find some drinkable tea.'

On Sunday evening, Vi sat on the balcony of her hotel room waiting for Stephen to return. He had driven off in the van to find a beach, as he had done the day before. She was worried about him. He was bored. But for her, he would not be engaged on this long journey so beset with delays. He might not be returning to England at all. She would have to make it up to him, recompense him in some way, but how? Not with money. Apart from paying for all the expenses of the journey home, she could not afford to give him any sum that would be worth giving. Even if she could, she would not. Money would not be good for him. She would think of something – something that she valued and that he would value.

It was half-past six. In the street below, a lorry was passing slowly by, laying the dust with jets of water sprayed from a tank. A couple on a motor-bike swerved past. They both had long wavy yellow hair which streamed behind them. They wore leather jackets and trousers. Two pairs of tall leather boots were strapped to their luggage on the pillion. That was how Stephen should be travelling. They pulled up at the customs building on the far side of the road. They would be leaving tonight.

The rays of the weakening sun appeared in fits and starts, filtered by the leaves of trees, a fistful of Guy Fawkes sparklers. Beyond, a strip of sea was visible between the quay and the hills on the far side of the bay. It looked like a piece of silk stretched taut across a stage and shaken to simulate rippling waves. A small car ferry was backing out, its engine guttural, like catarrh. A man padded his way past the customs building and through a small public garden which was divided into sections by box hedges. He was holding his hands behind his back as though to balance his paunch. From his hands hung a white polythene bag.

Violet watched from her balcony. As the sun sank, the street filled. People came to the café opposite and soon most of its tables were occupied. Still Stephen did not return. Had the van broken down? She had noticed on Friday that it had been missing on hills. She hadn't liked to call attention to this as Stephen himself had not mentioned it. Waiters were weaving their way between the café tables as gracefully as dancers. She had spent her life waiting, and watching other people doing things. 'I'm not mentally deficient or a cripple,' she heard Stephen say.

The paying guests could be counted as work, surely?

'I shall take in paying guests,' she had told Betty and Arthur in India. It was not something she had thought of until that moment. She hadn't realized then that she would have to think about money; nor that these thoughts would prove so unsettling. When she returned home and talked to the family solicitor, it was a shock to discover that her income would be so small. 'Your father did live on his capital all his life,' explained the solicitor. 'It's not surprising that it has come to this. And as I made clear, I believe, before your visit to India, your sister has the bulk of the stocks and shares. My advice to you is that you sell the property.'

This she would never do. Instead she placed advertisements in the *Lady*, and for the next ten years a steady stream of visitors stayed at the house. Betty did not approve. She complained about the 'awful people that roam all over the garden'. By this time, Betty and Arthur had at last built their house but they had no justification whatsoever for their complaints. They rarely came home on leave and, when they were away, their house was let in their absence. What was the difference between their awful people and hers? Besides, none of them were awful. And they were company. Some stayed long periods. Others returned time and again. There were only a few who caused problems and usually these were the ones who were high-handed with the staff. Then Violet would spend hours smoothing the ruffled feathers of Cook, or Elsie, or Nanny Burton, or one of the ever-changing housemaids. 'I don't know what your mother would've said,' Cook would say on these occasions. 'She'd never've allowed the likes of *this*!' But only the housemaids came and went. Cook and Elsie and Nanny Burton stayed on. They all enjoyed it. Violet would sometimes join them in the pantry and they'd exchange stories about the guests. Some stories were repeated time and again. The one of Mr Fawcett's toupee was a favourite. Nanny Burton had seen this lying on his pillow as she placed the early-morning tea tray on his bedside table. She had killed it with her bare hands thinking it was a mouse. Then there was the time that Mr Evans fell in the pond. He'd been stalking Mrs Milverton, a high-spirited widow. This was Sam the gardener's story, brought inside and embroidered by those in the kitchen. 'And 'e was tittuping up behind 'er on those 'igh 'eels of 'is . . .' There was Miss Kingdon who had done amazing things to her natural north-country pronunciation. 'I'll have a slice of that harm, it will do me no ham.' Elsie, whose aitches were irregular, was particularly fond of this one. 'It's arm today, mardam,' she would tell Violet, and they'd both laugh at the memory of Miss Kingdon. Long forgiven was Elsie's betrayal over the semolina pudding.

How well they had all got on. Those were the days . . .

Brought to an end by the war.

'Oh dear,' said Vi. 'This is my last pill.'

She and Stephen were eating their evening meal. Stephen had at last returned from his expedition and, after a shower so fast that Vi doubted its value, escorted her to a taverna recommended by someone he had met on a beach. The taverna was in the process of being built. Six tables were set in a space formed by a grey cement skeleton. On three sides bricks filled the gaps between the cement pillars. The bricks looked as though they had been thrown there. Until such time as the haphazard nature of the brick-laying could be forgotten under plaster, strips of yellow, green and red plastic hung on one wall. However, the barbecued chicken was delicious. It was brought from a kitchen across the alleyway where skinny cats lurked, watchful and alert, as predatory as rats.

'Do you think I should try and buy some more?'

Stephen had no answer to this. How was he to know?

'I wonder if I ought to ask a doctor . . .'

After a short silence Vi said, 'I don't suppose you remember Doctor Doolittle.'

'Yeah,' he said. It had been on television just the other Christmas.

'You always wanted me to read you the bit about the push-me-pull-you.' Unlike Diana and Elizabeth, who had lain in bed giving her their rapt attention, Stephen had fidgeted and interrupted. He had been most particular about what she was to read and what she was to skip. It hadn't been nearly so enjoyable reading aloud to Stephen. Elizabeth had had such trouble getting him to go to bed in the first place and once there, he had seldom concentrated on the story for more than a few minutes, jumping out of bed to fetch a watch or a toy to fiddle with.

'Oh, the book. No, I don't remember,' said Stephen.

'You used to love aeroplanes,' Vi went on. 'All your favourite toys were aeroplanes and then, when you were older, you used to make models of planes. Just like Tom.'

Stephen leant across for Vi's half-finished plate of chicken and chips. She pushed it towards him and sat back. 'That was surprisingly nice,' she said, 'for such a strange place. That's what it reminds me of, an air-raid shelter. Though ours wasn't like this a bit. Ours was very low-ceilinged. It had been the place where we kept ice. It was built into the steep bank behind the house. There was just room for all of us: Nanny and myself, Betty and the girls, sometimes Arthur. We had a paraffin stove down there and a kettle – in fact, it wasn't unlike having tea in your van the other day. I thought there was something familiar about that. Yes.'

'Were you bombed?'

'No. There was nothing in the town to make us a target. But a couple of bombs did fall not far away. Planes off course, or being chased, dropping their load before going back across the Channel. We could see London burning in the blitz. The whole sky was lit up.'

'Oh, Mum's told me about that.'

'Heavens, she was tiny! Does she remember that?'

'I don't know whether it was the blitz but she's talked of seeing the sky lit up. And the noise of the planes going over. And the – what were they called? The missiles?'

'Doodle-bugs.'

'Sort of missiles, weren't they? I wouldn't have minded being alive then. At least something was happening. And with war in them days you had a chance. Not like now.'

'Not like now, no.'

'Was that when you had your bike?'

'That was later. After Nanny died.'

Some of his friends called their grandmothers Nan. 'But she didn't die till after I was born.'

'Oh no, she died in 1943. Then I joined the WVS.'

'Who was Nanny then?'

Vi began to explain. She wished she could tell Stephen everything about Nanny, about the family, the house, the life she, Violet, had lived. But so much of it had been lost beyond recollection. Besides, Stephen was not interested. It was like Doctor Doolittle all over again. After a few moments, he pushed back his chair and asked to borrow money for the evening.

'Oh *Stephen*, not again surely! We have to be up at half-past four in the morning. The agent said we should be there an hour before the boat leaves. You must get a good night's sleep.'

'I can sleep on the boat.'

Stephen had met an Australian girl on the beach. She had said she would look out for him this evening. She would be in a bar called the Blue Lagoon. He had liked her. She had liked him. She was travelling on her own. He wanted to find the Blue Lagoon but, without money in his pocket, there would be no point.

He eyed his great-aunt carefully.

'No, Stephen. I am not going to give you a penny. You must come back to the hotel.'

She sounded unusually resolute. He wondered if he might tell her about the girl. He could perhaps make out he was lonely and bored. Once he had gained Vi's sympathy, he would tell her he had the brief opportunity to alleviate this melancholy state of affairs. She would understand that he could not meet a girl without money in his pocket.

He sat down again and heaved a great sigh. 'Oh, I'm pissed off,' he said.

'What was that, dear?'

'On me own the whole time. Part from you that is.'

'Oh I do understand, Stephen. It really is so good of you –'

'I was bored on the beach but then I saw this bird.'

'Really? I didn't think you were interested in birds.'

What did she think he was? Stephen wondered.

'Was the beach sandy?' Vi was asking. 'Was it by the water's edge? Long legs? A wader possibly. You should have taken the binoculars.'

'I didn't need binoculars.'

'You got close then? What colouring?'

'Blackish-brown with blue eyes.' Perhaps old spinsters were interested in this sort of thing. Stephen was willing to be interrogated for the sake of a possible hand-out. 'With very long brown legs,' he added for good measure.

'A summer visitor, I expect.'

'Yeah. Not a local. From Australia in fact.'

'Oh no. Not possibly, Stephen!' Vi laughed. 'Migratory birds seen here are travelling between Europe and *Africa*.'

Stephen sat back. The thought of untangling this one was too much. He gave up the idea of an evening out. In any case, if they did manage to get past the customs in the morning, there would be little point in seeing the Australian tonight. He walked back to the hotel with Vi, listening to her pondering the identity of a long-legged bird with blackish-brown plumage.

He wished they had not chosen a hotel directly opposite the customs building. Every time he had caught sight of it during the past two days, he had been reminded of the difficulties that could lie ahead. Vi seemed to have forgotten all about this, which suited Stephen. He had been spared the added worry of her worry.

However when, at five o'clock the following morning, they joined the queue of cars to go through customs, Stephen decided it would be wise to prepare his great-aunt. 'I'll do all the talking here,' he said. 'You just stay put.'

It was still dark but in the lights of the shed ahead Vi could see that the passengers of the vehicles in front were getting out, leaving the drivers to edge forward. 'No, dear. I can manage. Give me the documents and I'll get out to deal with it all when we're a bit closer.'

'No, Vi,' said Stephen firmly. 'I'll do it.'

Vi glanced at him, surprised by his tone of voice. She remembered her passing thought that he might be involved in smuggling something. Surely not!

'The tax business,' he said. 'Dates and stuff.'

'Oh heavens, yes. I'd quite forgotten.' She plucked nervously at her handbag. 'Oh dear.' Now she felt as though she herself were trying to smuggle something through customs. Her face grew hot and her hands sticky. 'Even so, Stephen,' she said after a while, 'maybe it would be better if I got out with the papers. An elderly woman like myself . . . ? They won't bother to look too carefully, will they?'

Stephen finally agreed. They edged forward slowly, eyes on the movements of the officials, police, people and vehicles ahead. A policeman appeared round the side of the lorry in front of them and waved vigorously at Stephen.

'Oh dear,' said Vi. 'What does he want?'

The policeman banged on the bonnet of the van.

'He wants you to open the bonnet. Get out, Stephen.'

'Oh shut up, Vi. He just wants me to join the other queue.'

'But we were directed into this queue. The other queue may be for another ferry.'

'He can see our sticker.' Stephen leant out of the window and shouted, 'Ionian Glory?'

The policeman repeated his bangings on the bonnet and his elaborate gestures. Stephen released the clutch too fast, the van shot forward and stalled. The policeman jumped out of the way just in time. 'Oh Stephen!' Vi had her hand on her heart.

'Shut up will you and *help*! Can you see behind? I've got to reverse to get round this lorry.'

Vi strained to see out of the window. 'I think you've got room,' she said.

'Think! Have I or haven't I?'

'Oh dear.'

Stephen jumped out of the van to have a look for himself.

'Oh dear,' said Vi again when he climbed back in.

'Look,' he said as patiently as he could, 'you get out now with the papers and join the queue.'

'Where is it? I can't see –'

'Over there. Ask. You'll find it.' He thrust a bundle of papers into her hand and leant across to open the door. 'And you'll need your own passport, don't forget.'

'But what shall I say?'

'Nothing!'

He heaved a sigh of relief when at last she was out of the van and he had joined the line to which he had been directed. This line, he now noticed, was composed of only three other vehicles, all campers of one description or another and each one empty. Why had he been sent here? Where was the policeman? Where were the other drivers? Should he get out? Join Vi?

He leant back in his seat, folded his arms and closed his eyes. Vi was right. It was best that she dealt with this.

Vi had found, and joined, the queue that shuffled along towards passport control. On her left she could see through a window into the office where a girl was riffling through one of many boxes of filed cards. Vi felt an urgent desire to talk about her and Stephen's possible predicament. She turned to the couple standing behind her.

'Chilly at this hour of the morning, isn't it,' she said. *Say nothing!*

'Ya, ya.' Both the man and the woman smiled encouragingly. They came from Munich, Vi discovered, and visited Greece every year. 'Now that Gerhard is retired, we come for one month, sometimes two,' the wife elaborated.

She mustn't say that Stephen had been here for six months. 'I knew a Gerhard once,' she said. The Shah of Balham . . .

Vi realized she must have spoken her thought aloud for the couple were talking about a niece who lived in Balham. 'Do you know Balham Park Road?' the wife asked.

'No, I live in Surrey.'

'Your friend lived in Balham then.'

'No, in Putney.'

'Our niece has to pay sixty pounds a week for her very small flat. London I think is too expensive nowadays.'

'It always has been,' said Vi. She had taken the five-pound piece from her jewellery case hoping it would buy her a flat in London! What innocence! Now that five-pound piece had become a blue van in which Stephen had spent too long in Greece.

'My nephew –' she began.

'Is he the one in Balham?' they prompted.

'No, he lives in Surrey too.' Through a gap in the line of

cars nearest her, she glimpsed a section of the van. The cars moved forward a yard or two and now she could see Stephen. He was sitting slumped in the angle between his seat and the window. He seemed to be asleep. 'There he is, over there.'

'That is nice,' the woman said. 'You are on holiday with your nephew.'

They were nearly at the counter. Vi clutched the papers. 'Yes, on holiday together.'

'Just the two of you? So you must have a good relationship. What is that expression? Get on? Get on well.'

'Yes, we do get on well,' said Vi. Did they? Perhaps they did. Last night, as they approached the hotel, Stephen had suddenly told her that the bird on the beach had been a girl. They had begun laughing at the absurd misunderstanding. For some reason their laughter had escalated far beyond its origin. She hadn't laughed so helplessly for years. Stephen had only to say 'wader' to set her off again.

She smiled. And now he was so relaxed about her ability to cope with the officials that he was having a snooze. 'Yes,' she repeated, 'we do get on very well.'

A moment later both her passport and Stephen's had been stamped. How easy that had been! She only had to point at the van to show where Stephen was. Beyond that, not a question, not a word.

She said goodbye to Gerhard and his wife. 'Perhaps we'll meet again on the ferry.'

'But next is the customs,' they told her. 'For the car documents.'

'If your nephew is the driver, then he must be there,' said Gerhard.

Now it was Vi's turn to wait in the van while Stephen dealt with the papers. He wanted her to come with him but she said that the strain of getting through passport control had been enough for her.

Stephen joined the queue at customs, wondering how Vi had ever managed to travel on her own before. She seemed to have no idea what was going on at all. She'd been triumphant about 'getting them through', as though passport control was the hurdle. He found himself almost hoping that he had overstayed his permitted time. That would show her. He wouldn't mind having his departure delayed. He could go to the Blue Lagoon.

On holiday with your nephew, Violet heard the German voices say. How good that sounded. It had only been the whitest of lies to let them believe this. Circumstances demanded such a side-step. Had she embarked on an account of how she and Stephen came to be travelling together, she might have found herself talking about the six-month limit right in front of the passport controller. That would not have been very clever. She had managed well – but now she sat in the van feeling guilty. 'I have washed my hands,' she told Elsie. She felt as uncomfortable now as she had done then. The years between the seven-year-old imitator of Tom and the eighty-six-year-old traveller with Stephen had been spent rigidly adhering to the truth, the whole truth and nothing but the truth. Stories in the *Telegraph* of deceit and falsehood upset her considerably. When a government official was discovered to be embroiled in an elaborate lie, she felt as mortified as she would had it been a member of her own family. Today even those in power could not be trusted to tell the truth. And today, she herself was sitting in a van that might be stuffed with drugs, trying to slip out of a country without paying a tax . . .

When she saw Stephen returning accompanied by a policeman, she all but fainted. However, she managed to take a firm grip on herself and rally to Stephen's aid. She leant out of the window. 'Officer, officer,' she gasped as they drew near, 'we thought it was six calendar months! And the delay was all my fault. I can explain.'

Stephen was making extraordinary faces at her.

The policeman opened her door. 'Please. Out.'

'You see, I developed carbuncles –' She pointed at her leg as she climbed out.

Stephen grabbed her arm in such a way that she swung round to face him. He mouthed 'shush' and then in a loud voice told her that the policeman just wanted to take a look inside the van. Once the policeman had climbed inside, Stephen whispered, 'It's all okay. Don't say a word.' Then he was called into the van by the policeman who wanted him to open a jammed cupboard door.

Violet waited anxiously. A second policeman joined the first. Both back doors were opened and things tumbled out onto the ground. 'Oh Stephen,' Vi whispered to herself, 'what have you got me into?'

Cars moved slowly past her, their occupants staring curiously. The German couple were in one. She could barely bring herself to return their wave. She noticed Mrs Gerhard craning her head backwards to take another look.

A hand on her elbow made her start out of her skin. The first policeman stood beside her. Was she being arrested?

'No problem, Mrs,' he said. 'In now. Good journey.'

'There were three certain things in my young days,' said Violet, settling herself on a bench. 'God, the King, and Father.'

On her lap she held the binoculars which she had brought up on deck. It was half-past seven in the morning and the car ferry was approaching the harbour of Corfu. The sun's rays lit the castle on its promontory.

'We were fortunate,' went on Vi. 'We knew where we were.'

Stephen sat down beside her. He tried to follow her train of thought.

'Nowadays nothing is sacred,' she went on. 'Everything is questioned. Perhaps that is a good thing. But it's unsettling. It's like living on a quagmire. What, for instance, do you believe in?'

Stephen rolled himself a cigarette. He liked conversations which roamed over such questions: what does it all mean, where are we all going, why are we here, is there life after death and is there life in outer space. He could go round and round these subjects for hours on end, but never at seven-thirty in the morning. He had come up on deck for a lie-down.

'Not much,' he said. He thought perhaps he should do better than this. 'Nothing, in fact. What do you mean, believe in?'

'I mean, having faith in the existence of something that can't be proved.'

'Like God. But king and father? They were there all right, weren't they?'

'Yes, but what I suppose I meant by lumping the three together was their authority, their infallibility. Their word was law. We did what we were told. It was so much easier. Policemen, for instance,' she went on after a pause, 'policemen were people you could trust. They were on your side. That business at customs this morning – well, it reminded me of the war. Did you notice he was armed? He had a pistol in a holster.'

'They all do,' put in Stephen. 'That's normal.'

In 1943, after Nanny Burton died, she had gone to live with Ivy and do her bit for the war effort.

'My friend in Chamonix,' she began, but Stephen was at the rail. The ferry was nearing the quay and he wanted to watch the goings-on.

It had taken her forty-three years to leave home. No, perhaps that was unfair; say, twenty-three years of adulthood. Had she been like Ivy, then she would have left in her early twenties. But how could she, Violet, have done this, against the wishes of her parents and without money of her own? She had no skill or talent to offer the world. Ivy had thought her feeble.

'All right, so you've joined the WVS,' said Ivy, lighting yet another cigarette as they drank tea at the kitchen table. 'But that doesn't mean you have to sort woollies for the rest of the war. I hear they need relief drivers at the

Ministry. You're a good driver. Why don't you apply for that?'

Ivy worked in a very secret department of a very secret organization. All Violet knew was that she pedalled off on her bike at half-past seven every morning to a country house with a garden full of prefabricated huts, and returned, looking white and haggard, at half-past seven at night. Sharing a flat with Ivy was not the fun that Violet had expected. There were no parties. Even at weekends Ivy often worked or went away. But Vi made her own friends. She bought the motor-bike. In fine weather, instead of making the occasional visit home by train, she went by bike. She brought back vegetables from the Lodge garden which Betty's ancient gardener was now looking after. Her vegetable casseroles made with lots of Marmite were popular with her new friends. They were women of her own age who lived in the town and, though they came from varying backgrounds, they discovered they had much in common – mainly their delight in their new sense of purpose.

Those two years in the flat were the best of Vi's life. She revelled in the hardships of power cuts, rationing, black-out, air-raid warnings, making-do. She loved sitting in the flat's kitchen, drinking tea and talking. She liked nothing better than to be called out at night to lend a hand at the incident post or to meet a party of refugees at the station and arrange billets. She took to wearing trousers, and only the voices in her head were shocked.

'We meet again!'

Vi looked up to see the German couple. Gerhard had been interned in the war. He had returned to England in 1937; visiting professor of economics at London University, Ivy said.

'You had trouble at customs, I think,' the present Gerhard was saying.

'Oh yes. I mean, no. They were just checking.'

'We have been chatting with your nephew.'

Gerhard made this sound ominous. An interrogation in a cell. Violet felt momentarily confused. This pleasant, friendly couple had been on the other side.

'Do sit down,' she said. Ivy's Gerhard had not been on the other side, merely treated as such.

'May I introduce ourselves? Gerhard Nothelfer and my wife Jutta.'

'And I am Vi Sharpe.' She made room on the bench.

'Your nephew says you have come from Petropolis. I was there in the war.'

'Military Attaché,' said his wife proudly.

'I was very young, of course,' said Gerhard with a smile. 'My first appointment. Do you like the Greek land and its peoples? We love them.'

The German couple entertained Violet with stories of their travels for some time. They too had visited Kenya, but on safari only a few years ago. Vi said, 'I was there just after the – in 1946. It was my brother-in-law's last posting. Army. Luckily he retired just before the Mau-Mau troubles.'

They knew Italy well and recommended a hotel north of Brindisi. By this time Stephen had joined them again so they gave him precise instructions where to find the small town of Fasano.

'The hotel has a lock-up garage. That is most important in Italy, particularly in the south.'

Then came a cautionary tale of a friend who had had everything stolen in Brindisi. He had not been careless. He had parked his car right outside a restaurant so that he could keep an eye on it while he ate. Yet when he looked outside having paid his bill, his car had gone. He had only a little money on him. Everything else, including his passport, was in the car. Instead of continuing his journey, he had had to return home with the help of the German consul.

Violet's hands gripped her handbag. 'We must get to this place with the garage, Stephen. I hope there'll be time tonight?'

Gerhard assured her that, if the ferry docked on time,

they should be there by eight o'clock. 'We ourselves are going to drive all night. We take it in turns. So now, if you will excuse us, we must sleep.'

'Oh dear,' said Vi after they had left, 'that does sound worrying.'

'I can always sleep in the van,' said Stephen.

'So you can.' If such well-travelled people as Gerhard and Jutta drove all night to avoid staying in southern Italy . . . 'But I don't think I like the idea of staying in a hotel on my own.'

'I reckon they just want to get back fast. Nobody's going to want to steal my van in any case. Hey, hand over the binoculars. Let's have a look at Albania.'

'Albania?' Vi had had no idea they went anywhere near Albania. She wasn't even sure where Albania was.

'Yeah, over there. We're going through the Corfu straits, it's only a couple of miles wide. A bloke I was talking to just now said that people get blown out of the water round here, if they get too close. A couple of underwater fishermen were shot the other year. 'Course, they shouldn't have gone over to that side, their own bloody fault.'

'What can you see?'

'Nothing much. Pretty bleak. Something that might be a gun emplacement. Yeah, and another. Sort of slit in the hillside. Back of that bay I can see what look like blocks of flats. Yeah, blocks of flats. Grim. Stuck on the hillside. Like barracks. No balconies. I can't see any movement. Not like Corfu. Let's go round the other side and have a look over there.'

Vi reached for her stick. 'Gracious me,' she said, 'I forgot to bring my stick up on deck! I must be improving.' She got to her feet. 'I am a bit stiff though. Give me your arm, there's a dear.'

They were passing the northernmost point of Corfu. Against wooded cliffs below the blue-grey peak of a mountain, the sails of wind-surfers billowed like a line of brightly coloured washing.

Stephen handed his aunt the binoculars. 'There's one of them balloon things going up,' he told her, guiding her hands in the right direction.

'It's very dark and fuzzy. Oh no, that was your arm.' She altered the focus to suit her eyes. *There's one of them balloon things going up.*

A red and white shape swam into view, skimmed over the sea towards her, and then lifted high into the air. From a harness below dangled a figure. The balloon drifted lazily across the sky.

'Has it got an engine?' she asked Stephen. 'How is it moving?'

'It's being dragged behind a boat. See the boat? That's paragliding.'

'Have you done that, Stephen?'

'Only once. I got to know a bloke running one. He gave me a free go. Couldn't afford it otherwise.'

'I had a friend once whose interest, passion, was airships. Have you ever heard of the R101? It crashed at Beauvais in France on its maiden flight. He was on it.'

Vi handed the binoculars back to Stephen and went down to find her cabin. Lying down on her bunk she composed herself comfortably to think of Patrick.

She was sitting on deck with Gerhard and Jutta. Patrick was leaning on the rail. He was wearing a sports jacket. No, that would be too hot. A blue shirt would suit his eyes. The lock of crinkled hair that often fell over his brow would be blown back by the breeze. In profile the deep indentation between his broad forehead and his straight nose was accentuated. His mouth puckered at the corners when he was amused. He seemed to carry around with him a subterranean lake of amusement that threatened to break surface at any moment through his thin lips. Yet he rarely laughed himself; he just caused laughter in others.

'Let me introduce you to my husband.'

Patrick turned and looked at her quizzically.

Violet tried to make him shake hands with Gerhard and

Jutta who were now standing at the rail with their hands held out. Patrick's elbows still leant on the rail, his hands stayed clasped. He would not straighten. His weight was on one leg, the other casually crossed over it. On his feet he wore highly polished brown leather shoes.

'The grass is very wet,' said Mother. 'You'd better wear galoshes.'

Vi said she would bring them round to the French windows. 'I'll find a pair large enough.'

'Size ten or thereabouts,' said Patrick.

He had come to lunch. Now, having finished their coffee, Father wanted his nap. Mother would retire to bed again, and Violet would show Patrick the summerhouse which had been built down by the pond.

Violet's galoshes scrunched on the gravel. She found Patrick sitting on the seat outside the morning-room windows, waiting for her.

'I hope these will do,' she said.

'But I only need one.'

She looked down at the pair she had laid on the gravel in front of him. The faded black rubber feet seemed to mock them both: Violet for her obtuseness, Patrick for the enormous space where his right leg should be.

She could not move or speak.

'I only need the left one.' He pushed his left shoe into the rubber casing and, leaning forward, ran a finger around the heel until it fitted. Tucking his crutches under his arms, he stood up.

'I wonder what the singular is. Galosh sounds quite absurd. So. Aren't we going for a walk?'

She still could not move or speak.

'Come on, Vi. Don't be so upset. You'd just forgotten which one was missing, that was all.'

His way of excusing her made it worse, not better.

'Let's go,' he said. 'In any case, I'm flattered you had forgotten my pathetic state.'

She followed him, her inability to break her silence embarrassing her still further.

'You are a sausage,' he said. 'If I had a spare arm, I'd put it round you. Come on. Tell me about this summerhouse. Did your papa have it built for his bird-watching? A kind of glorified hide?'

The questions hung there, waiting for her answer. 'No,' she said. 'He had it built' – she felt the tears coming – 'in memory of the boys.' She wept. 'I wasn't crying for the boys,' she said as she recovered in the summerhouse. She blew her nose again on Patrick's large white handkerchief. He had been telling her about Tom's last days, something she had wanted to hear from him ever since their first meeting. Presumably he thought it would help her at this moment. She had thought it would, too. But now she found that she did not want to hear about those days of war. She did not want to be able to imagine Tom in the cockpit of his aeroplane, that flimsy structure with its failing engine, its fireball of flames. Patrick, in fact, had been talking not of this but of the songs in the mess and Tom's piano-playing. Vi wanted her memories of Tom to be kept intact, not muddied by images of scenes she had not shared.

'I wasn't crying for the boys,' she said again. 'I don't any longer. They were part of my childhood. Now I'm grown up. I've made myself think of them in the same way as I remember, oh, I don't know, birthday parties, or favourite dolls, or punting on the pond in a makeshift boat – things that can only happen when one is a child. One can grieve for such things but you grieve for them because they are past and unrepeatable, not because they are missing from the present. I know I don't make myself clear. I am so hopeless. That's what was upsetting me. I do not seem to be able to do anything right. Here I am, grown up. I'm twenty-one! I used to think it would be such fun to be grown up. Everything would be possible. And here I am doing nothing more exciting than making sure Mother has her beef tea!'

Patrick was silent for a moment. Then he spoke of Ivy. Her

sister was now married. Perhaps Violet might consider taking her place in Ivy's London home. 'I'm sure she'd love to have your company. You could go to art school. Those landscapes of yours –'

'They are wretched. Victorian watercolours! Father has more talent than I have! And I can't leave home. Mother needs constant attention.'

'The house is full of people waiting on her hand and foot.'

'They need organizing. They need to be told.'

'No one is indispensable.'

'I couldn't afford it. I have no money of my own.'

'Your father could pay for you.'

'He would never do that.'

'How do you know? Have you asked him?'

'I wouldn't dare to ask him.'

Patrick said nothing.

'Besides,' went on Violet, 'I don't think I'd like to live in London. I always come home with the most dreadful headaches after visiting Ivy.'

'Probably that's because of those vile cigarettes she smokes. I wish she wouldn't.'

The smell of smoke in the cabin roused Vi.

Stephen was telling her that it was time for lunch.

'I wonder what happened to the pond,' said Violet.

All had been well at Fasano. The van had been safe in the lock-up garage. The food had been good, the beds comfortable. Refreshed, and excited at the prospect of this new leg of the journey, they had made an early start and rejoined the main road by half-past nine in the morning.

'And the summerhouse,' she added.

On either side the land lay flat and dull. Olive trees grew from red earth. Prickly pears edged stone walls. There were advertising hoardings all the way along the road. Violet could not stop trying to read the signs: *Tatarella, Bellice, Pizzeria, Ristorante, Rallantare* . . . Each new sign appeared before she had fully read the one before. *Miali, Martina.*

A pink-washed villa appeared on the right and then was gone.

'How strange. It had steps on its roof leading nowhere.'

Stephen bent his head towards her. 'Sorry? I can't hear you.'

The noise of the van drowned his voice. The engine roared, the body rattled.

'These bloody Mercedes,' he said. 'They come up right behind you flashing their lights. Come on, Bess.'

'I was wondering what happened to the pond,' repeated Vi much louder. 'The pond!'

'What pond? That's the sea!'

The road had been running parallel to the coast for some time. Between the road and the sea was a string of buildings. Some were possibly holiday flats, others warehouses or factories.

She would ask Stephen about the pond when they stopped. Conversation was impossible. *Zona Abitata*. Grand Hotel d'Arra something. Arragona possibly. Why Arragona here? There was a small green Deux Chevaux in front of them. She didn't think it was a very good place to pass. The back of the little car was plastered with stickers: place-names, messages, and two – ?

They had passed it. She hoped Stephen would not take many risks like that. For one thing, the van seemed to lack acceleration. Two little ducks, white and black with red beaks. *Our* van, she thought, is much more original.

Although the sun was hidden by a high haze, it was growing hot in the van. She had tried opening her window a crack but this made it even noisier. Perhaps they could stop soon for a lemonade.

'Perhaps we can stop soon for a drink of some description?' she suggested.

'This must be Bari we're getting near,' shouted Stephen. 'Look out for signs. Those green ones.'

'A14?'

'South, Pescara, Taranto and Napoli. Do we want that?'

'Do we?'

'Look at the map!'

Violet fumbled for her glasses and the map. 'We want Pescara but we don't want Napoli.'

'Look for more signs.'

They were on the outskirts of Bari, being whisked past blocks of flats, pylons, a waste area of rubble and refuse, a vast yard of stacked yellow crates.

'Right! Go right!' called Vi. 'Pescara we want. Pescara and Napoli together, going right.'

Stephen seemed to hesitate but turned in time. 'Good, there's an autostrada sign. We'll be joining it in a moment.'

'I thought we'd been on it all along,' said Vi. Then she noticed a sign. 'It says *NO Autostop*. The no in capital letters.'

'That means no hitch-hiking on the motorway.'

'Oh of course. I thought it meant it wasn't the motorway.' Things happened so fast, there was no time to take them in. If Stephen would only slow down a fraction . . . *Bari Zona Indust.*

Stephen had slowed down; in fact to a halt. They were at a barrier.

'Your side,' he said. 'Take a ticket.'

'Do we have to pay then?'

'Just take a ticket.'

'Where from?'

'Press that red button and a ticket comes out.'

'Isn't that neat,' said Vi when she had eventually managed this. 'It must save such a lot of time. And labour, not having a man here.'

Stephen made a rude sign to the queue of cars hooting behind him.

'Oleanders, how pretty.'

At any moment, thought Stephen, she'll suggest we stop for a picnic among the shrubs in the central reservation.

Here! Here! They had all taken turns in shouting but Dad never stopped in time. Choosing places for picnics had taken ages. Aunty Vi was often with them. Round the time Stephen was seven or eight, probably. They stopped going on family picnics by the time he was in his last year at primary.

Picnics had been great. He had liked having the whole family together and out of the house. Being out of the house made everyone much more good-tempered. His sisters hadn't squabbled on picnics as much as they had at home. They'd even played with him. Aunty Vi used to sit on the tartan rug and be the one person who stayed there all the time. You could come back and talk to her on your own without other people telling her what you were wanting to say. Mum had played cricket with them, sort of French cricket with family rules. Dad had taught him how to spin a ball.

How had his father managed to find the time to come with them? Had he been less busy then? He had been on his own. It was much later that he had formed a group practice with the other two. Was it because he had wanted to spend time with his family in those days, when they were still young enough to be ordered about?

They'd found some smashing places for their picnics. The ruined abbey covered in ivy. That boathouse on a lake in the middle of woods; probably private but no one had come along. The high round hill where they had flown kites and where he had felt part of the sky. Mum had been good at picnic food. Sardine sandwiches. Sausages rolled up in bacon. Sometimes chicken drumsticks. Always a cake. Would they be home in time for Sunday lunch? It was now Tuesday. The last time they'd phoned, what had they said about their return? Had they given a date? No, Vi had told him not to say anything definite. They would call again when they reached the Channel.

He noticed that Vi had become two different people in his mind. There was the Aunty Vi of the picnics, the great-aunt of his sisters and himself. And there was the Vi of this journey. He no longer thought of her as his great-aunt. He had even, without realizing it, stopped calling her 'Aunty Vi'. She'd become ageless. Certainly there were things about her that were irritating – mannerisms, ways of talking, slowness – but these things he found irritating in the way he might find a friend's habits irritating. And, now he came to think of it, there were many people who annoyed him far more frequently than did Vi. He'd rather share this journey with her than with anyone else he could think of. Even Jake, on the journey out, had proved to be a selfish bugger. You really get to know what people are like, he thought, when you travel with them.

When they stopped for lunch, he must ask Vi about that airship friend of hers and the R101. He'd seen a programme on airships. Massive great things like ocean liners in the sky. Crashed at Beauvais. Had they all been killed? Was that why there was no 'Uncle Vi'?

'Your friend in the R101,' he said as they tackled large ham rolls in the car park of an autostrada service stop. Vi would not leave the van to eat lunch inside. She suspected everyone of being a Mafia car-thief.

'Patrick,' she supplied. It gave her a thrill of pleasure to tell Stephen his name.

'How did he get to be on board? I thought it was its maiden flight – without passengers. Was he a pilot?'

'He was an Army pilot in the war, yes. But not then. He had lost a leg. How they ever let him on board, I never could understand. But then he was Irish.' She said this as though it explained everything. 'There *were* passengers. Lord Thomson – he was the Secretary of State for Air – was the VIP. He was going out to India. He'd been keen on the idea of airships for a very long time. And then there were other air officials on board, I believe, but no members of the public. Patrick got on as a journalist. He wrote articles on aircraft for the papers and he was particularly fascinated by airships. He planned to write a book about them. He was the kind of person who could talk his way into anything. And of course Thomson and Sefton Brancker and all the others who thought airships the answer to modern travel – they were all keen to get good publicity.'

'Were they all killed?'

'No,' said Violet. She could hear the announcer's voice. 'Of the fifty-four passengers, there were only eight survivors.'

'And Patrick?' asked Stephen, already guessing the answer.

'He was not one of the survivors.'

There was a short silence. Stephen was the first to come up with the change of subject they both felt was needed.

'We were bloody lucky to get past customs yesterday,' he said.

'Why?' asked Violet nervously. Was the van full of heroin after all?

'All those drachmas you were smuggling out.'

'*What?* Me, smuggling? What do you mean?'

'You had hundreds of pounds' worth of drachmas in your bag, didn't you?'

'Well, yes. What was wrong with that?'

'You're only allowed to take about thirty quid's worth out of the country! You must have had four or five hundred in your bag!'

'Oh, Stephen! Thank heaven you didn't tell me at the time!' She thought about this for a moment. 'But they let me change them into lira on the boat without much trouble.'

'That's different. That's just a banking service, nothing to do with the customs police.'

Violet felt quite faint at her escape. 'What about the next border then? Italy to France? Will we – will I have to smuggle again?'

'I don't know about the Italian regulations. Best not to. Just breeze through like you did last time!'

'Oh but Stephen . . . I wish you hadn't told me.'

'Innocence in the sight of the law is no excuse. Or whatever the expression is.' He laughed at Vi's dismay. 'Now what about a cup of tea?'

'Not that dreadful camomile.'

'No, the Igoumenitsa version of Tetley's.'

When they were once more on the road, Violet remembered her question for Stephen about the pond and the summer-house. The summerhouse would certainly not have survived the property development. But the pond must surely still exist. Perhaps Stephen had even played there as a small boy.

Until now she had never thought of wondering whether the pond still lay in its hollow somewhere among the rows of commuters' houses. In her mind the old house and its grounds still existed on the hill above the town; but this hill was somehow quite unconnected with the hill on which the Winfields lived, their redbrick house echoed a hundred times with only minor variations among the winding tree-lined roads.

After the war the house had been in such a sad state of disrepair that she had finally taken Arthur's advice to sell up. She could not afford to put it to rights. Nor, it seemed, could anyone else. A year passed. She watched the growing pace of decay from the Lodge. When eventually someone made an offer, she accepted it gratefully even though the solicitor said it was far too low. The purchaser was a Major Cummings.

'An Army officer,' Vi told Arthur and Betty. She was as delighted by the news as they were. It would be a relief to see the house rejuvenated.

'Has he a family?' asked Betty. There might be friends for Elizabeth and Diana.

Vi didn't know. She had met him only once. He had come to the Lodge for the keys, which he had then kept to save her trouble. The sale went through swiftly. Workmen arrived. From the Lodge Vi could hear them at work. She watched a lorry drive away laden with fireplaces. So they were putting in central heating. That was sensible. It had been such a cold house even in the days when there were maids to light the fires in every room. The next lorry drove away piled high with doors. This was puzzling. There had been nothing wrong with the doors beyond the need for a coat of paint. The kitchen dresser shared a lorry with bath, basins and a conglomeration of lead pipes. Vi walked up the drive to the house, her curiosity now far stronger than her desire not to appear curious. The workmen were on the roof, passing slates from one to another.

'Excuse me,' she said to a man who appeared to be in charge, 'but what is happening? The roof is perfectly sound. We only had a slight leak in 1923 or so and it was well repaired at the time.'

'It's all right. We're saving the slates. You can get a good price for slates like these.'

'Saving the slates? They seem to be taking them off completely.' There was a large hole in the roof above the nursery window.

'That's right, one at a time. Major's orders.'

'So he's having a new roof? That seems an awful waste of money to me, though I know it's none of my business.'

'No, no, the whole place is coming down. We're just saving the good stuff. Then it'll be over to the demolition gang.'

If the man had pummelled her in the ribs, she would not have felt as sick.

She walked shakily back to the Lodge. She had thought that Major Cummings had fallen in love with her house! But he was knocking it down. She would not tell Betty this yet because she knew exactly what her reaction would be. She would approve of his plan to build a new house. Betty had no feeling for the past. 'Quite right, too, if he can afford it,' she'd say. 'All mod cons.' This was one of her favourite expressions.

By the time Vi reached the Lodge she had decided what she would do. She rang the estate agent. Six months later she had moved to the cottage with a fraction of the furniture which had been in store. The Lodge and the rest of the furniture she sold. That Christmas she felt reckless and rich. Instead of spending it with Betty and family as usual, she went to America on board the *Queen Mary*. She stayed away for three months, missing the worst winter in living memory. Betty was furious with her.

Stephen, slowing down to join a queue of cars stopped at a red light, noticed Vi's amusement.

'Just thinking of your grandmother,' she explained. 'Isn't it strange how some people always feel badly done by. They think others are so much better off than they are themselves. Betty was always convinced that I was the lucky one.

She envied me my freedom and independence . . . What's this hold-up?'

They were now moving slowly through a tunnel.

'An accident?' Stephen suggested absent-mindedly. He was thinking that his mother viewed Aunty Vi as the rich relation. Had she inherited this impression from her own mother? And was it false?

'Oh dear, so it is,' said Vi. At the far end of the tunnel, men were waving red flags. Beyond them a blue car lay on its side, crumpled. Behind it lay another, also crumpled.

'How dreadful,' she said, turning away. She hoped the sight of such destruction would make Stephen drive at a more sensible pace.

It did. For a while, the traffic moved along in a cowed and law-abiding manner and Vi was able to ask her question about the pond.

'You mean the pond at the bottom of Acacia Drive? 'Course it's still there. I helped make it.'

'You can't have done. It was there when I was a child. We used to row on it.'

'The only pond I know about is the one we made. It was a project in Environmental Studies. We spent weeks shifting a whole load of rubbish. It was called the Pit and it was the place people chucked things. Prams, mattresses, old cookers and fridges, all half sunk in this bog. It stank. Once we'd cleared it, they got a digger in and then we planted stuff. We had our photo in the paper for that.' He pointed at the shelf in front of Vi. 'Somewhere at the back there's a compass I found in the Pit. Caked in mud but apart from that it was in pretty good nick. Still works too.'

Vi leant forward and searched among the maps to find the pocket compass that her father had given Tom. She held it level in the palm of her hand and watched the needle steady itself.

They were driving due north.

'If we have time,' she said, 'I would like to visit Beauvais. It's not far from the Channel ports.'

Beauvais? That was where she'd said the R101 had crashed. 'Right,' said Stephen. He thought of the man Violet might have married and regretted, for her sake, his death. His grandmother, Betty, had had her family. Violet, no one.

Stephen was driving fast again. He overtook a lorry on the back of which was painted a large red mouth with a long tongue curling from it. *Materiale di construzione,* read Violet, her eyelids growing heavy. The landscape had become more interesting and the sky a clearer blue. Bumpy hills, and the scooped-out valleys in between, were patterned with squares of ploughed earth, blocks of sweetcorn, rows of vines and dots of olive trees. The road swept through the hills in tunnels and over the valleys on stilts. *Uscita* meant exit. Tonight she would see if she could remember any Italian. *Per favore.*

Ivy had sent her a card from Rome. 'We go on to Florence tomorrow.' She never did discover who had turned Ivy from I to we.

That was in 1929. Her visit to India had given her the taste for travel. The first flurry of paying guests was over and there was a longish gap before the next ones were due. Ivy suggested a holiday in Italy and saw to the booking of the tickets. A week before departure she telephoned. Would Vi please be her usual, decent, understanding self and back down? Something had cropped up. They would definitely go together another time.

The postcard from Rome was a surprise, for Violet had understood from the telephone call that the trip was off for both of them. But Ivy had gone, and with someone else. She was hurt but told herself that perhaps the 'we' meant that at last the shadowy figure hinted at by her friend over the past few years was growing more solid. Soon she might even be told his identity.

Ivy had always been secretive about some areas of her life.

When Violet had gone up to London to turn the five-pound piece into freedom and independence, she had called in at Ivy's house. She had not warned Ivy in advance for the day had not been planned.

'The egg is soft,' said her mother, her head propped forward by three embroidered pillows. 'You know I cannot abide sloppy eggs.' She pushed the tray away.

Violet left the room without a word, her heart beating in her chest. She did not go down to the kitchen to remedy the matter of the sloppy egg. Instead she telephoned the most willing of her mother's friends and asked her to call in during the morning. Then, taking her seventh birthday present from her jewel case, she took the train to London.

She bought the *Evening News* at Waterloo and, over a cup of tea in the station buffet, pencilled asterisks beside all the flats to let in the Holborn, Clerkenwell and Bloomsbury areas. The columns were soon speckled with stars, for Violet had set herself no price limits. She had little idea how much she might need to acquire a flat and set herself up in it, nor how much the five-pound piece might fetch.

She took a cab to Sotheby's. She was directed to the right department by a series of young men who managed to combine an obsequious manner with a powerful aura of superiority. Vi had arrived in London in a mood of energetic determination. By the time she reached a door marked 'Coins and Medals', this mood had vanished. She had gained the strong impression that these young men spent their time dealing with young unmarried women wishing to sell possessions of doubtful provenance, for purposes of which they would certainly not approve. The five-pound piece was examined under a magnifying glass and deemed to be in good condition. It could be entered in the next sale which would take place in two months' time. Did Miss Sharpe wish to put a reserve price on it? Once this had been explained to her, Miss Sharpe thought that she did. How much? She had no idea. Twenty-five pounds was suggested.

'But there was an article in *The Times* . . . It said that gold . . . I had thought . . .'

'Unless you have an urgent need, I would suggest that

you keep the coin for many years yet. With items of this description, it is rarity which gives the value. There are still many such pieces around.'

Vi wrapped the coin in its tissue paper. She would leave her bid for freedom and independence for another year. Twenty-five pounds, although it seemed to her a princely sum, would not be enough to pay for a flat and support her until she could support herself.

It was midday. She did not want to return home just yet. She would visit Ivy and perhaps even stay a few days in what had been the sister's room. Mother would just have to manage without her.

She walked up Bond Street, looking at the women in smart hats and furs sitting at counters being served by women in black dresses with neat white collars. Shoppers and assistants alike wore bright lipstick and their hair was dressed in the latest fashion. They moved with ease and assurance, waving their hands gracefully as they nodded, smiled and talked. Vi felt dowdy and hopeless.

In Oxford Street there were groups of girls walking along the pavements arm-in-arm. Perhaps they worked in offices, and this was their time for lunch. By the time she reached Ivy's house, she felt about ten years old.

Ivy came to the door.

'Vi! What *are* you doing here?'

Vi was taken aback by this greeting and her friend's expression which was far from thrilled. It had not entered her head that Ivy might be busy. She had even forgotten that the room vacated by the sister was now a studio where Ivy took portrait photographs.

'How stupid of me,' said Vi. 'I should have telephoned first.' She was still standing on the step. The door was not opened wide enough for her to enter. Could it be that she was not going to be invited in? 'Mother drove me mad this morning,' she continued. 'I came up on an impulse.'

Ivy hesitated for a moment and then stood back, holding the door open. 'Well, come on in.' She ushered Violet into the small front room which was seldom used. 'I have someone here. For a portrait. But I can spare ten minutes or so – they won't mind. I'll be down again in a moment.'

She closed the door as she left the room. Violet could hear her hurrying upstairs. There were footsteps in the room overhead and muffled voices. One was Ivy's; the other, a man's.

Violet sat down at a round table by the window. The table was covered in a paisley cloth which Vi had seen on several occasions draped round Ivy's shoulders. A leather-covered album of photographs lay on the table. Perhaps this was to show prospective customers. Violet turned the leaves slowly, examining each photograph in turn. Heads turned towards her; fine-featured women with wide eyes beneath arched eyebrows; men with glasses, men with pipes; two small curly-haired children. Then there was a photograph lying face-down between the next two leaves. Violet read the words pencilled on its brown paper mount: Friedrichs-hafen, 12th October 1924. ZR3.

She looked up as Ivy entered the room.

'Are these all yours? They're very good.'

Ivy held a bottle of wine and two glasses. She crossed the room swiftly, put the wine and glasses down on the table and snapped the album shut. 'You don't want to look at that rubbish,' she said. 'Tell me about Mother. Is she being more of a pain than usual?'

Vi described her day.

'Twenty-five?' exclaimed Ivy, when Vi reached Sotheby's. 'You should have put it in the sale, you duffer. You could do an awful lot with twenty-five pounds.'

'I don't think so,' said Vi. 'I don't want to take any risks. If I do leave home, I want to make sure I don't starve.'

'You wouldn't starve. We'd make sure of that!'

Vi understood this plural referred to their friends in general. But on her way home she heard the 'we' again. She had visited the bathroom before departure and seen on the shelf above the basin a shaving brush.

*

'Where is this?' asked Vi.

They were driving slowly in heavy traffic through a system of flyovers and underpasses.

'Bologna,' said Stephen.

Vi looked at her watch and was disappointed to see that it was only half-past four. She had been hoping it was time to stop for the night.

'We *have* come a long way. You must be awfully tired, Steve.'

He felt warmed by her concern and by the name. She had not called him Steve before.

'I'm fine,' he said. 'But I'm not sure about Bess. She's missing a bit on hills.'

'I'd noticed that,' said Vi. 'But I thought she was doing better today.'

'She's all right when we are going along steadily and the road's flat.'

'Perhaps we should stop in an hour or so.' Vi put on her glasses to study the map. 'We might find a village off the road somewhere. Let's see if I can recognize any of these place names. Ivy and I did this part on our way from Rome and Florence to Venice. Modena, Parma and Verona, we went to. Modena, yes I've found it. Not far from here. We stayed in a very nice hotel somewhere between Modena and Parma. I wonder if it was in Reggio?'

'How long ago was this?' asked Stephen, expecting the answer to be close to a century.

'Not long. Let me see. It was soon after Betty died. About 1974 perhaps.'

He had been seven. He suddenly remembered Aunty Vi on his seventh birthday. She had sat on the sofa telling him that seven was a very important age. He had thought her extremely old and extremely odd. He laughed at this idea and at the fact that it was the same woman sitting beside him now.

'I suppose that seems ages and ages ago to you,' said Vi,

assuming that this was why he was amused. 'To me it was only the other day.'

Ivy had made a good travelling companion. She still took photographs and with her camera drew Vi's attention to things that would otherwise have gone unremarked: a water melon echoing the shape of a sun umbrella, an old man's face beneath a gargoyle, hay draped on poles looking like fairground candy floss.

'Look at that,' said Steve. 'You'd think they'd be more mechanized here.'

Stephen had said this earlier in the day as they drove through hilly country where hay was drying on poles.

How odd this was. At the time Stephen's remark had not reminded her of Ivy's photographs of hay. But remembering Ivy's photographs had recalled the remark of an hour ago. The past was reminding her of the present. In fact, past and present seemed inextricably confused. Perhaps this was the result of the long day's drive. For a moment she could imagine that she and Steve were stationary and it was the landscape that was moving. She wondered if time could play a similar, illusory trick.

A long hour later, they turned off the autostrada towards Parma, Stephen having resisted Vi's desire to wander the back roads from Modena to Parma in search of the hotel she had stayed in years before. But despite this resistance, they found themselves in a back road after all. Tiredness, confusing signs, and Vi's inadequate map-reading had led them to a narrow, deserted road which crossed an empty, flat, agricultural plain. On the far horizon the grey shapes of a small town with a tall bell-tower appeared on a hump of land.

'Can that be Parma?' asked Vi uncertainly.

'Far too small. And look where the sun is. We must be going north-east. God knows how we've done this. Parma's west of the autostrada.'

'Well, it doesn't matter, does it? All we want is a place to spend the night.'

The small town turned out to be little more than a large village but it did have a hotel.

'Per favore?' Vi enquired through the bead-curtained front door. Stephen, glad that his aunt was willing to do the talking, looped part of the curtain aside so that she could peer into the dark interior. Just inside the doorway two old women sat on chairs, side by side against the wall. They were dressed in black and wore black headscarves. On their laps they held white enamel bowls full of long-stalked leaves. Their bony brown hands stripped the leaves from the stalks and tore them to shreds. They did not look up.

'Per favore,' Vi repeated, more loudly. *'Avete delle camere libere? Per una notte. Due persone, due camere singole.* I think that's right. Ivy and I often had trouble getting a single room each but that might have been due to the hotels' architecture, not to our bad Italian.'

The women had by now looked up but still did not speak. Their eyes went from Vi to Steve and back again.

'Maybe they're deaf,' suggested Vi at this lack of response. 'Maybe they are nothing to do with the hotel.'

'Maybe this isn't a hotel at all,' said Steve.

Vi tried again, less ambitiously. *'Patrone? Dove patrone?'*

At this one of the women opened her mouth and let out a shriek. Vi stepped back.

'Well, that got a reaction, didn't it,' said Steve.

A man appeared at the far end of the hall and, after an excited exchange with the two old women, ushered Vi and Steve through a door and up a dark stairway. He limped ahead of them, occasionally stopping to turn and gaze at Steve. This was disturbing for only one eye focused on its object. The other swivelled wildly as though attempting to see behind its owner.

Three doors led off the landing. The patrone opened all three. The first revealed a room with four single beds; the second, a lavatory with a shower; the third, after a struggle to push it open wide enough, a vast double bed and a single couch.

'Well,' said Vi. 'It looks as though we will have to take over the entire hotel to acquire two single rooms.' She threw her handbag onto the double bed and turned to the proprietor. '*Quanto costa?*'

Stephen left her to discuss the price for two people using rooms that could sleep seven and went to fetch their bags. When he returned, he found her sitting on the side of her big bed laughing weakly. She had found a tourist leaflet, no doubt left by a previous occupant, in a drawer of the Odeon-style dressing table.

'You must read this, Steve. But at suppertime. I shall have a short rest. Why don't you go out and look for a possible place for us to eat? Or are you desperately tired? I should think you are, after that long day.'

'Only tired of driving. I'll go for a wander.' He hesitated for a moment at the door.

'You have to pull it really hard. It sticks,' said Vi.

'I was just wondering . . .'

'Oh, of course. Money.' She gave him a couple of notes from her bag. 'Is that enough?'

It would have to do. Stephen tugged at the door and managed to drag it across the hump in the shining blue plastic-tiled floor.

He did not like having to ask for money all the time. After all, he was earning it. Vi should pay him weekly, a regular wage, as a matter of course. How much was chauffeuring worth? As he made his way down the stairs and past the two old hags who were still at their task of tearing weeds, he calculated that he should be paid the equivalent of a hundred pounds per week.

It was only after he had circled the village to discover that the only spark of life was in the triangular piazza which the hotel overlooked, that he realized that a weekly wage from Vi would be no help at all. They had only been together, he worked out to his surprise, eleven days. Not even two weeks! They would be home in less than a week. If Bess continued to go as well as she had done today, they could be at the Channel by Friday. This would be exactly two weeks after his arrival in Petropolis. Yet he felt as though he had been travelling with Vi for months. This wasn't because the time had dragged. On the contrary, now that arrival home was not such a distant prospect, he found himself wishing that the journey would last much longer. He liked being with Vi. And what was there to look forward to at home? 'So what are you going to do now?' he could hear his parents ask.

On the far side of the piazza there was a pizzeria and next door to it a sign advertised a *ristorante*. As he crossed the square to compare menus and prices, he became aware of the attention he was attracting. All the people in the village under the age of twenty-five had gathered by the central fountain. They were dressed in what Steve termed trendy clothes. They seemed to have nothing better to do than watch him walk by. Suddenly it was hard to remember how to walk. What happens to arms, for instance? Where do you put them? If they swing at your sides, do they swing in time with your feet? Left arm and left foot forward? Or left arm and right foot?

Steve made a swift decision. There was no need to choose an eating-place just yet. He and Vi would do that together later. He turned and walked, as best he could, back to the hotel.

The staring trendies were still there when he walked back with Vi later in the evening, but this time it was only Vi who paid them any attention. He was more interested in the stories she was relating of her friend in Chamonix.

'How nicely dressed they all are,' said Vi. 'Of course Italians have terrific style.'

'Was it on television?'

Vi thought he was talking about Italian style.

'No, the programme on your friend. Ivy.'

'Oh, that. Yes, it was for television. But I don't think it's been shown yet. I think Ivy told me it will be on this autumn. A series on women photographers. I hadn't realized she was famous. But then, I don't think Ivy did herself. The television people went out to Chamonix in the spring, she told me, and interviewed her on a chair going up Mont Blanc. Very cold and very uncomfortable. She said they were fed up because she's destroyed so many of her early photographs, so they had to do something interesting with her. I would have thought they could have found something *warmer*. She's older than I am.'

'Now you must read this funny thing,' she said when they had chosen both their eating-place and then their meal. She found the leaflet in her handbag and passed it across the table to Steve.

He turned it over lazily in his hands.

'The bit in the middle there. The Palio of Asti,' she prompted.

'All this? What's funny about it?'

She watched him begin to read slowly, a frown on his face. He was even mouthing the words! She reached out and took the leaflet. 'Oh goodness me,' she said, 'if it's as hard work as that! I'll read it to you. Though perhaps it won't be so funny. What probably happened was that someone with a good grasp of English wrote the translation by hand and gave it to a printer who couldn't read his writing. I'll have a go.' She began to read in a soothing, story-telling voice.

' "The tradition of the Palio of Asti originates from the Middle Ages" – you see, it starts in fine style, lulls you into thinking all is well. "The first historial record, dating back to 1275, mentions the Palio as a tradition aready wen establisched at that time. Since then on the First Saturday in May, the ceremony of the stima of the palio, the precious hanner –" '

'Hanner?' asked Steve.

'Hanner. Banner.'

'Oh, banner.'

' "The precious hanner awarded to the winner, takes

place. On this occasion the Mayor publicly announces the Palio of that year –" '

'Should Palio be something else?'

'No, I don't think so. I think that's just an Italian word.'

'And what's Asti?'

'Asti's a place.'

'Oh yes. Near Turin?'

'Yes.' Was this going to fall quite flat? It did get better. She would hurry on. 'Where was I? Oh yes. "The Palio is one of the most important and ancient Italian historical traditions that heeps the atizens of the carions rival quarters of Asti busy au year, in the zeal of creative work, historical rearch and parties." ' She glanced up to see Steve's expression. He was peering towards the kitchen quarters but, noticing her pause, turned and smiled.

'Carrion's rival quarters?' he asked.

She spelt out carions. 'Various,' she said. ' "During the days before the race the tension and suspense build up. Great banquets ave organized in the street and squares of each quarter and attended by the untrabitants and fareign fquests." '

'Untrabitants! And fareign who?'

'F-quests. Hard to say.'

'We are fareign f-quests. I like being a fareign f-quest.'

Vi felt relief. Steve was getting into the swing of the prose. She continued reading, warming to her task. ' "The main events of the day before the Palio are the traditional 'Mercatino' with its stau with the colours of each quarter, and in the ofternoon the presentation of the horses on the course of the Palio. On the marning of the theird Sunday in September, day of the Palio, the groups of sb –" oh, I can't pronounce this.'

'I wonder,' said Steve, 'how long fareign f-quests have to wait for their food.'

'Their fond.'

'Sorry, their fond. Or their fool. That would be better.'

' "*Sbandieratori,*" ' continued Vi, ' "create a colourfield backgron to the anquie –" ' The waiter appeared. 'Ah, at last,' she cried, flinging out her hands towards him. 'The fool!'

'Madam?' asked the waiter, who spoke excellent English. Stephen burst out laughing. Vi struggled first with her embarrassment, then with her laughter.

The waiter seemed anxious to understand their amusement but, as neither of them could for the moment speak, he laid their food on the table and left to watch them from the sanctuary of the kitchen doorway.

'Oh these fareign f-quests. Their minners!' said Steve in an Italian voice.

'Minnows?' Vi managed at last to ask.

'Manners, middim.'

'Stop it, Steve. We must stop! This is not good for me at my age. It's ridiculous. Oh dear me!' She blew her nose loudly on her handkerchief. If Steve continued, she would have to ask for the ladies and who knows what that would be like in a place like this. 'Do you think,' she asked with great solemnity, 'we will reach Chamonix tomorrow?' She looked at Steve, willing him to answer normally. Their eyes met and she knew her effort at control was in vain; even the most innocuous words sounded absurd. But how lovely it was to share such an eruption of laughter.

Looking back, the next day's drive was their best, yet it was not the one they remembered most vividly for it was uneventful. It merely passed pleasantly. They both felt relaxed, content with each other's company and with the present moment. The van, for the better part of the drive, gave no sign of trouble. Once they had passed Milan, there was less traffic generally and in particular fewer heavy lorries to harry them. The heat was not so intense but the sun was still warm. Before setting off they had gone together to shop for picnic food, and this they ate at midday in the shade of poplars by a stream, a place they found without making a long detour from the autostrada. Over lunch, urged on by Stephen's questioning, Vi talked of her life and the people she had known. She was surprised by his apparent fascination.

'But it's awfully dull,' she said. 'I've never done anything of any importance.'

Stephen hunted for words to explain why he liked to hear her talk.

'I mean,' went on Vi, 'think of the times I've lived through: the first war, the General Strike, the Jarrow marches, the Spanish Civil War, the –'

'Oh, I'm not interested in history –'

'All the things that have happened, all the changes. I can't tell you anything of any significance. I'm not clever. I can't, oh I don't know, sum up, teach you, pass on . . .'

'Do I want to be taught?' asked Steve, smiling.

'I think not.' She smiled back. 'I'm like that bird over there, that lapwing.' She pointed across the stream towards a lapwing that was picking its way over furrowed earth, its beak to the ground. 'A revolution could be going on in Milan and what would it know about it? I've just lived. And I've been lucky that nothing awful's happened to me personally.'

'Your brothers. That chap, what was his name, Lejeune? The one who helped Patrick into journalism. You said he was killed in Spain, in the Spanish Civil War. Your friend Ivy, having a television programme made about her. All that sort of stuff.' And he had thought that Vi was just an old relation who lived in a nearby village and who had sometimes come on picnics with them and who had, he could just remember, sold poppies on Poppy Day.

'Oh, yes, other people. I certainly knew some interesting people.'

'But it's you who are talking about them. You make them interesting and even if they weren't . . . Perhaps everybody's interesting when they're talked about.' He started clearing up their picnic, putting scraps of paper into the largest paper bag. 'Any rate. We ought to be moving so that we reach Chamonix and your *interesting* friend this evening.'

He helped Vi to her feet. 'No stick again today?' he asked.

'Yes, isn't that good? The wretched things have cleared up.' Vi kept an eye on the paper bag of rubbish in Steve's hand and was pleased to see that he did not throw it in the stream. Instead, he tossed it into the back of the van.

They set off once again, in the somnolence of early afternoon. The land lay flat on either side of the road, farmland broken now and again by plantations of poplars, isolated factories and old farmhouses with faded tiled roofs and high archwayed barns where giant coils of hay lay stacked like piles of oversized gold sovereigns.

Both Vi and Steve were puzzled by dark grey circles that every so often swirled from the tops of poplars by the road.

'They're flies, I think,' said Steve at last. 'Swarms of flies or bees.'

Vi's eyes were closing. 'I thought they were balloons,' she said. 'Balloons of smoke . . .'

There's one of them balloons going up.

Who had said that?

Sam rested his foot on his spade and leant his folded arms on the handle. He looked up into the sky as though he would see the 'balloon' he had read about. It was a trial flight of airship R101 from Cardington and the article that Sam had read in the paper had been written by Patrick.

Vi told Sam this but he was either uninterested or, more probably, unwilling to believe that someone who had visited the house and whom he himself had seen was responsible for words printed in a newspaper. Sam believed that everything he read in the newspaper was a personal message from the All-Knowing, All-Seeing God. ''Twas in the paper,' he would say to confound any disbeliever of the information he imparted. He was proud of his ability to read and all the papers that came to the house were passed on next day to the Lodge. Here they were read and enjoyed far more thoroughly – and, moreover, kept. When Vi moved to the Lodge, she found them filling one of the bedrooms. 'Not an inch of floor left,' she told Ivy years later. 'Stacked to the ceiling! Like that Cronin story.'

Ivy asked if she had kept the papers and was cross to hear she had not.

'But how could I possibly keep them! They took up one entire bedroom!'

'You could have sorted out the really interesting ones. There'd have been the ones that –'

'That what?'

'That were printed during the General Strike,' answered Ivy with a rush of inspiration.

Vi realized that Ivy had been thinking of some other reason for not destroying all the papers. It made her wish that she had kept the ones in which Patrick had written articles. She would have loved to reread his words. His style had been so vivid; you could almost hear his Irish voice as you read.

There's one of them balloons going up. That was not Patrick's voice, nor was it Sam's. It was Steve's. They were looking across the sea to Corfu. Now they were on their way to Chamonix. Balloons went up in smoke. There were a lot of accidents.

Patrick suggested lunch at the Trocadero in celebration. 'I've wangled my way onto the India flight! I'm to be ready at a moment's notice.'

He had taken her to lunch at the Trocadero once before. That had been a previous celebration about another airship. He was being sent to Germany to cover the launch of a giant passenger Zeppelin. 'Have you heard of Dr Hugo Eckner?' he asked. 'He's the great Zeppelin man. He came up with the idea of giving an airship to America in lieu of reparations. Brilliant! The ZR3 is going to cross the Atlantic!'

'Will you be all right on the journey?' asked Vi anxiously.

'*I'm* not going on the flight,' he answered with some amazement.

'No, I meant on the boat and the train to Germany. Is it very far? Whereabouts in Germany is this launch to take place?'

'I shall be perfectly well looked after. I'm going with – with a photographer. Once we've crossed the Channel, the train will take about eight hours. It's in the south, a place called Friedrichshafen on Lake Constance. German–Swiss border, in the Alps.'

'Vi! Toll!'

'Where are we?' asked Vi, fumbling for her bag.

'Aosta. End of the autostrada. The Valley of the Aosta and the beginnings of the Alps.'

'Of course, they all thought then that balloons were the thing.'

Stephen glanced at his aunt. Did she realize she had been asleep two hours? Sometimes she showed her age.

But she was now fully awake and alert and he was glad, for the scenery had become stunning. It was good to share his excitement at the views with a companion. Craggy hills rose on either side, their angles caught by slanting sunlight. Vineyards on stone-built terraces were stacked in layers up the steep lower slopes. The vines were strung along wooden poles supported by stone columns. The road followed the course of a river. Smoky-blue water tumbled over white boulders. Every so often they exclaimed at the sight of a castle silhouetted on a bluish-grey pinnacle or a slate-roofed village caught in a gully like the debris of a quarry. The mountains rose higher, their peaks snagging clouds.

'I shall have to find a cardigan,' said Vi. 'This is the first time I've felt chilly for weeks.'

But Stephen did not want to stop. Bess had faltered a couple of times. 'Can you last till we reach the Mont Blanc tunnel? It can't be much further.'

The skyline was now so high, they had to bend their heads to catch glimpses of the peaks. The sun had disappeared behind white cloud. Ahead lay darker cloud towards which the road snaked its way.

'That's not cloud at all,' said Steve. 'That's Mont Blanc.'

Vi saw that what she had thought was sky was in fact a wall of rock swathed in cloud. She could see tiny cars and lorries zig-zagging up the wall. 'I thought you said there was a tunnel,' she said.

'Yes,' said Steve tensely. 'Haven't you noticed the signs? The entrance is in another few kilometres.' He put Bess into bottom gear, and when at last they reached the customs barrier at the entrance to the tunnel, he did not dare switch off the engine.

'They're waving us through, I'm not stopping,' he told Vi. 'You can find a cardigan when we get to Chamonix. It's no distance the other side.'

Vi was sitting with her arms folded close to her chest. 'That's all right,' she said.

'Just pay for the ticket here. Twenty-one thousand lira.'

Vi handed over the money. 'But what about exchange?'

'We can do that in a bank in Chamonix. Better, in any case, as you have so much.'

'Oh yes. Of course.' Vi began recalling their experiences at the customs in Greece but, to Steve's relief, her voice trailed away as they entered the tunnel. Perhaps it was the thought of the colossal weight of mountain above that silenced her, or had she noticed the engine was occasionally faltering and become as nervous as he was? His grip tightened on the steering wheel and he silently pleaded with Bess not to die in the tunnel. He counted off the kilometre signs, proceeding from one emergency telephone box and lay-by to the next as though he were playing musical chairs.

As they finally emerged into the light, he let out an enormous exhalation of breath. 'That was the longest twelve kilometres I've ever done!'

'Magnificent!' breathed Vi. 'What an excitement, going right through a mountain!'

'Just wave your passport again,' said Steve. 'We don't need to stop.'

He could see the roofs of Chamonix in the valley below.

'Just look at that!' exclaimed Vi. 'What is it?' On this side of the mountain the sun was shining brightly in a blue sky. To their left a brown and white jagged mess towered above the road.

'A glacier,' said Steve. At least the road was downhill all the way to the town. If necessary, they could freewheel.

'But what an extraordinary sight. It's so dirty, so prickly!'

Maybe he should have a go at cleaning the carburettor this evening. The danger was that he might make things worse, not better. Engines often repaid his attention in the most spiteful ways. Better to leave well alone. And Bess had done well. She had got them to Chamonix.

'Now what's the address of your friend?' he asked as they drove into the town.

'Oh, we'll leave that till tomorrow morning,' said Vi. 'We can't turn up on her doorstep tonight.'

Steve had assumed that they would be free-loading with Vi's friend. But it didn't worry him one way or the other. After all, he wasn't paying. This was a very good thing, he thought, as they booked into an extremely comfortable, extremely expensive hotel in the middle of the town. Vi assured him that she had plenty of money left. He only hoped her sums were accurate.

They ate their evening meal in the restaurant of the hotel as they had no francs. After paying thousands of lira for the most modest meal, Vi was inclined to think that seventy-five francs for the set menu must be extremely good value. Stephen thought otherwise. He even borrowed pencil and paper and attempted to work out what their final bill for dinner, bed and breakfast might be in English terms. Vi was touched by his concern but she thought it needless. Besides, all the additions, divisions and multiplications were spoiling her enjoyment of the *escargots* and *quenelles de brochet*. She finally made him stop throwing figures at her by promising to do sums of her own before she went to sleep.

But when she got to her room, she was too tired for this. They had drunk a bottle of wine between them and Stephen had not accounted for more than half. She opened the heavy double-glazed door and shutters onto the small balcony. Outside, the air was refreshingly cold. The moon hung large and white over the mountain above the town, lighting here and there patches of snow among the firs. Below the balcony, a section of brightly lit street was visible between the dark shapes of buildings. The voices of passers-by were just audible. Vi thought of Ivy. This was Ivy's town, Ivy's view. Perhaps she had drawn her curtain too, and stepped out onto a balcony to savour the moonlit night. Two old women, perhaps only a few hundred yards apart, staring at a mountain. Vi felt that Ivy was very close.

You'll catch your death, standing there like that. Either go in and go to bed or put on something warm. Did Stephen bring up all your luggage? It's about time you sorted out your clothes. Find the ones you left England in for the rest of the journey. That suit, for instance. That's warm.

Ivy's voice had always talked to her in managing tones, as though Vi were an untidy parcel that needed repacking before it could be entrusted to the post. Vi could see Ivy's hands smoothing out crumpled brown paper, wrapping it squarely around a box, folding the ends into triangles to make crisp corners, and finally tying string firmly round the parcel with a neat knot. *There!* Ivy's laugh was throaty and fond.

Of course, that was why Ivy ever bothered with her at all. It was her very hopelessness that Ivy liked.

What would she think of Steve? Vi looked forward to introducing them. She must make sure he wore the least bedraggled of his clothes and gave his hair a good brush.

I noticed the waiters giving him a funny look. But then, do you remember Anthony? He never brushed his hair and that was at a time when all the men had partings!

Vi turned back into the room, closing the shutters and the window behind her. The voices in her head continued until she fell asleep.

The next morning she woke Steve early, and over breakfast they discussed their plans. She would go to the nearest bank and exchange money while he found out where Ivy's street was. She wrote the address on a slip of paper for him.

'Ask the reception desk here,' she told him.

'Do they speak English?' he asked, looking rather anxious. Vi had dealt with all the talking so far in what sounded to him like fluent French.

'Of course.'

She returned from the bank with the news that they had

the equivalent of £258 left. 'And some chicken feed,' she added.

'But we'll never make it!'

'Surely we will,' said Vi confidently.

'I don't see how. Petrol, food, hotels, the Channel crossing . . . How much is our night here, for instance?'

Vi's expression was less confident when she returned from the desk. 'Well, we'll just have to be more economical from now on. No more smart hotels. We can always sleep in the van. There's probably only one more night in France, isn't there?'

'Or do you think we should borrow a bit from your friend? Just in case?'

'We could do that. Yes, that is a good idea. Have you found out where the flat is?'

Apparently it was within walking distance. They decided they would put their luggage in the van but leave the van where it was. 'We might not find another parking space,' said Vi. 'I shall take my stick.'

Stephen searched in the back of the van for his leather jacket. Although it would be a sunny day, the town was still in shadow. Vi was wearing a navy-blue suit and had wrapped a mohair scarf round her throat.

'I hope we shan't catch colds from this sudden change of climate,' she said. 'But the walk will do us good. Did they say how far it is?'

'Ten minutes or so.'

Half an hour later, having climbed the length of the wrong street, they found the right block of flats. Vi hesitated at the front door. 'Steve,' she began, 'perhaps it's best if I –'

'Fine,' said Steve. 'I'll wait here.'

'Just until she recovers from her surprise. After all, it will be rather startling for her, to find me standing on her doorstep.'

Steve pointed at a bench at the top of some steps opposite the building. 'I'll be there. Shout from a window or something.' He crossed the street.

Vi put on her glasses and examined the list of names beside a row of bells. She found Ivy's name and this gave her a thrill of pleasure. She pressed the bell and leant her head towards the grille of the entry phone. There was silence. Of course Ivy might have gone shopping . . . She pressed the bell again. Or become deaf? It was some years since she had last seen her. As she pressed the bell for the third time, the door opened and a woman appeared carrying a dripping mop.

'Oh,' said Vi. '*Bonjour, madame*. I have come to visit Mademoiselle Ivy –'

The woman was already speaking. Vi had a little difficulty with the regional pronunciation but understood that she was being asked if she came from England.

'*Oui. Je suis une amie d'Angleterre.*'

'*C'est bon. Je suis la concierge. Entrez.*'

The concierge opened the door wide and Vi went in, turning to give Steve a little wave as she did so. Stephen was sprawling on the bench with his legs stretched out before him and his arms spread-eagled along the back of the seat. His head was tilted back and his eyes were closed. The sun, now reaching this side of the valley, lit his face. In contrast to the pale-complexioned people of the town, he looked almost Indian. He'd told her that in Greece his headband had earned him the nickname of 'Red Indian'.

'You have received the letter from the solicitor then?' asked the concierge as she led Vi to the lift.

'Pardon?'

'You are the friend from England?' The concierge hesitated at the open door of the lift.

'*Oui, oui.*' But why 'the' friend? And what was this about a letter from a solicitor? 'There has been no trouble? Is Mademoiselle Ivy all right?'

'*Votre nom, s'il vous plaît*. There are several names on the list.'

Vi told the concierge her name. The lift door closed on them. The concierge pressed the button for the third floor. The mop made a pool of water by Vi's feet. Did Ivy perhaps have a list of friends who might possibly visit from England?

The concierge was muttering. 'I shall have to check. Sharpe. It was a longer name than that. But you are a friend?'

'Friends for almost seventy years!' answered Vi with a smile.

The concierge shook her head and sighed. 'Sad that you were not in time for the funeral.'

Vi felt her heart give a lurch. Ivy was not in her flat on the third floor. Yet last night on the balcony . . . Ivy had tricked her. She had seemed so alive, so close. It could not be possible that she was dead. 'Pardon? What did you say?' She might have misunderstood the concierge.

They had arrived outside the door of the flat. The concierge was fitting a key into the lock. If Ivy were alive, she would open the door herself.

'When was the funeral?' Vi heard a voice ask. 'When did she die?'

'Two weeks ago. It was sudden, a heart attack, but she expected it. She had begun tidying up all her things. I said, "But you will live to be a hundred, Madame!" She knew though. Look!'

Vi had been led through a small hall to a room made dark by closed shutters. The concierge switched on the light. The room's furniture was barely visible beneath cardboard boxes filled with papers.

As the concierge talked, Vi watched the mop drip on Ivy's carpet. Why had the woman not left it downstairs?

'There is a list somewhere here,' said the concierge, 'of people she left things to.' Vi joined her by a table. 'Ah, this is it. Is your name here?'

Vi held the sheet of headed writing-paper on which Ivy had written a list of names. Some of them were known to her. Most weren't. Her own was the third from the top. 'Vi Sharpe,' she said. 'That's me.'

The concierge breathed heavily beside her. 'Ah, yes. Then you have the box.' She handed Vi a flat yellow box of a kind which Vi recognized. Photographic paper was sold in such boxes. Its lid was held down by string from which a label dangled.

The concierge was watching her as though she were about to open a birthday present.

Vi tucked it under her arm. She wanted to leave straight away.

'*Merci, madame,*' she said several times as they made their way downstairs. The concierge was talking but Vi could not concentrate. At the front door she said thank you once again.

The door clicked shut behind her.

Then Stephen was beside her, taking her arm. They started walking down the hill.

'Was she out?' asked Stephen uncertainly. Vi's answer was not a surprise. He had guessed the news from his great-aunt's dazed behaviour.

'I'm sorry,' he said lamely.

'Oh well,' said Vi. 'We can't live for ever. She was eighty-seven. I shouldn't have assumed . . .'

Her voice was sprightly and her step had quickened.

'Actually,' she said, 'I'm surprised she lasted so long. She smoked far too many cigarettes.'

Back at the van, they settled themselves into their seats. Stephen had a look at the map and pointed out the route to Vi. 'We'll fill up with petrol in the town. What's the time?'

'Half-past ten.'

'Good. Not too late. We might get to Paris tonight.'

'Oh, we don't want to stay in Paris, do we? That's bound to be expensive.'

'Right. We'll see where we are when the time comes. Ready to go?'

'Yes.' Vi buckled her safety belt. 'Oh, we didn't buy any food for lunch.'

'Let's buy it somewhere else. This is a clip joint.' He switched on the engine. There was no sound at all. He tried again.

Vi glanced at him. 'Petrol?' she asked.

'Not that.' He turned the key several times. 'It's dead!' he exclaimed. 'What the hell's wrong with the bloody thing?'

'The battery?' Vi suggested meekly.

She watched him get out. He lifted the bonnet, peered at the engine briefly and came to her window. 'Could you get into my seat and turn the key a few times?'

As she went around the back of the van to the driver's side, she looked ruefully at the two hands painted on the back doors. 'I'm not going to be able to push, Steve,' she called towards the bonnet as she got in. 'We'll have to get help.'

She turned the key in response to Steve's waving arm but it was clear that there was not a spark of life in the engine. 'It's not even making that struggling noise,' she said to Steve when he appeared at her window. 'It must be something worse than a flat battery. You'd better go and find a garage man to come and have a look.'

'Couldn't you go? I'll stay here and tinker.'

'No, I'm far too tired after that long walk.'

'But they may not speak English,' he said.

'Then you'll have to speak French. You've only to say you need help and bring someone back here.'

'I can't speak French.'

'Didn't you learn it at school?'

'Yes, but I can't speak it.'

'Gracious me, what do you mean? What *do* they teach you nowadays?'

Steve walked off rather than listen to a diatribe on education. He found a garage some distance away and after a wait and some elaborate miming, succeeded in securing the services of a mechanic with a breakdown van who drove him back.

'A breakdown van!' Vi exclaimed on his return. 'What is this going to cost!' She climbed out of the driver's seat and began talking with the mechanic excitedly. 'He's going to give us a jump-start,' she reported. 'Then we are to drive to his garage where he will look at the engine. That is, if the jump-start works.'

It did. But when at the garage Steve was asked to switch off the engine and then restart it, there was the same lack of response as before. The mechanic told them the van needed a new generator. He could order a generator by telephone and it might be delivered the following day, which was Friday. He would be able to fit it on Monday. Vi and Steve looked at each other in dismay.

'Ask him where the generator comes from. Perhaps we could go and get it.'

'How could we go and get it?' asked Vi.

'Oh,' said Steve.

But the mechanic had understood this exchange. He suggested that this was in fact a possible alternative. Annecy was under two hours' easy drive away. If Steve kept the engine revving well and did not stop or stall, they could get the van to Annecy. He would telephone the supplier there, and they would fit the generator on the spot.

It did not take Vi and Steve long to decide that it was worth the attempt. They both felt anxious to leave Chamonix.

'How much did that little lot cost?' asked Steve as they drove away, engine roaring. They had filled the car with petrol besides paying for the mechanic's help.

'Oh please don't talk, Steve. Just concentrate on driving.'

'There's a toll coming up. Have the money ready.' He used the handbrake at the barrier so that he could keep his foot on the accelerator. Vi, to his relief, was ready with her window down to take the ticket. For the next two hours they exchanged not a word.

The mechanic had given Vi the address of the garage in Annecy and detailed instructions on how to find it. They had reached the final roundabout when a car, swerving too closely to the van's wing, made Steve brake sharply and stall the engine.

They both sat back, almost relieved that what they had

been expecting so tensely to happen had at last happened. 'No,' said Vi with a smile in response to Steve's expression. 'I can't push. I'll steer. That's our road on the left. It is almost downhill.'

It was fun to sit at a steering wheel again. If ever it became necessary, she would gladly drive for Steve, even though she had no licence. How high one sat above the road. How easy it was to see around. What a pretty street this was, with its little villas and pollarded trees. So French! And yet so like – Putney!

'Turn! *Turn!*'

She realized that Steve had been shouting at her for some time. They were opposite the narrow entrance to the garage. She pulled sharply on the wheel. How heavy the steering was in a van. She only just managed to pull the van round to get past the entrance posts. Ahead a narrow road led down to a workshop.

'Brake! Brake! *Brake!*'

She could hear Steve's commands but she thought she ought to get the van right to the workshop before she stopped.

The workshop was suddenly very close. She put her foot hard on the brake, and when this seemed to have no effect, she grabbed the handbrake. The steering wheel hit her in the ribs. She climbed out of the van, rubbing her chest but beaming with pleasure. She looked around for Steve and was surprised to see him some distance away, running fast towards her. When he reached the van he did not congratulate her as she expected, but bent to run his hand over the wing.

'That car at the roundabout didn't hit us, did it?' she asked.

'No. It was you who hit that post as you turned in,' he said.

'Oh sorry,' she said lightly. 'I can't say I noticed.'

*

A few hours later Vi lay on her hotel bed, her back well

bolstered by pillows so that she could see the lake from the open window. She felt disorientated and exhausted, as though she had landed after a dangerous but exhilarating flight in some fragile craft.

So many hotel rooms . . . She tried to recall their shapes and colours and place them in the journey's chronological order. One of the rooms had wallpaper which had peeled away in places to show eau-de-Nil emulsion behind. There were patches where the paper had been stuck back on with shiny sticking-tape. A bare light bulb hung from the ceiling. The floor was covered in bright blue lino tiles that rose in a ridge by the door. The room was dark and cold so it was not in Petropolis. In Chamonix her room had made her think of Versailles. The present room was simultaneously Mediterranean and alpine. It was just as expensive as the one in Chamonix. She had ordered another thousand pounds from England.

'One *thousand*?' queried Steve, astonished.

'To be on the safe side,' said Vi. But this was not really the reason. Her mood, in the bank, had been reckless and euphoric. Why penny-pinch any longer? On the telephone her bank manager's voice had been soothing and confident. A temporary overdraft was quite in order. She could arrange matters on her return. Why indeed worry? Why not cash in her entire capital so that she and Steve could really enjoy themselves? She wished she had done this at the start of the journey. They could have wandered home, even not returned at all . . .

The thought of resuming her life at home had quenched her euphoria.

As she lay in bed watching the sails of windsurfers skim across the lake, she recalled the events of the day and her strange mood of excitement. Ivy was dead. Yet she had not grieved. The van had broken down but she had enjoyed the difficulties and tension this had caused. She remembered Steve pointing out that she had grazed the side of the van. This had seemed quite unimportant at the time. The news that the generator would cost over a hundred pounds and take a day to fit had not disturbed her in the least; nor had the use of a taxi for the hour it took to find a hotel and a bank.

Perhaps she had been in a state of shock.

And what did she feel now? Tired, depressed, alone.

You may well be tired. But why depressed? You are not alone. There's Steve waiting for you downstairs. He wants to take you on a pedal-boat!

The pedal-boats were lined up in an orange row beneath the trees of a park not far from the hotel. They had seen them on their way to the bank.

She was not sad that Ivy had died. She had not seen Ivy for years. Ivy was still as much alive for her as she had ever been. Her voice mocked Vi fondly.

You've never felt sorry for yourself. Why start now?

Vi reached for the flat yellow box that she had placed on the bedside table. What had Ivy left for her? Photographs, probably. Perhaps a letter too?

'Violet Sharpe' said the label hanging from the string. It was warming to think that Ivy had written her name in the last few weeks. She had put her not at the top of the list, but third. Whereas Ivy herself would be at the top of Vi's list.

Her fingers could not manage to untie the neat knot of the string that held the box shut. She reached for her handbag and found her scissors to cut the string. As the lid was released, a pile of photographs spilled from the box onto her lap, like uncorked champagne.

The first photograph lay face down on top of the pile. There was something familiar about its brown backing and the position of its pencilled writing. She put on her glasses, noticing as she did so that her hands were trembling. She had seen this photograph before.

Friedrichshafen. 12th October 1924. ZR3.

She could see Ivy crossing a room swiftly and snapping an album shut.

We didn't want to tell you, said Ivy's voice as Vi turned the photograph over.

Patrick and Ivy, arms linked around each other's shoulders, leant towards the camera, laughing.

Stephen leant forward in the driving seat, straining to see the road ahead. The windscreen wipers were barely coping with the torrential rain.

It had still been summer in Tournus that morning. They had wandered round the street market choosing cheese and pâté and fruit for their lunch. Vi seemed more animated, after two days of unusual silence caused of course by shock at her friend's death. The business with the generator had merely delayed the reaction. Once settled into their Annecy hotel, she had virtually collapsed. The following morning he had finally persuaded her to let him take her on the lake in a pedal-boat. He'd been sure she would enjoy it. But she had sat there woodenly, quite unlike her usual self. He found himself looking at the view as though with her eyes, encouraging her to see what in normal circumstances she would appreciate. She did not respond. He returned the pedal-boat to its moorings well before their half-hour was up. He led her through the park, asking her to identify the magnificent trees. She told him the names in a listless voice: Wellingtonia, Scots pine, plane. She did not remark on the tubs of pink and blue flowers that decorated the alleyways. Nor on the window-displays in the cake shops with their arrays of meringues, mousses, flans, éclairs, cream buns. What a waste! They had not taken advantage of Annecy, a town that he'd have thought Vi would love. What a good time they could have had there, if her friend had not gone and died.

Perhaps the death of Ivy reminded her of the death of Patrick. Stephen was pleased with this idea. How perceptive, his mother would say. He wondered whether his mother knew about the man who might have been Uncle Vi. He suspected she did not. He knew Vi better now than she did, he was sure of that.

He drew out to overtake a car with three windsurfboards tied to its roofrack. How out of place they looked in the pouring rain.

Would Paris be as hard to get round as Lyons had been?

They had left Annecy in the middle of the afternoon the day before. The money had been telexed through with amazing speed, and the van was ready for collection by three o'clock as promised. They had reached the outskirts of Lyons at what was no doubt the worst time of the week, five o'clock on a Friday afternoon. The traffic had come to a virtual standstill. It took them two hours to edge their way round the sprawling immensity of the town. Vi had sat in silence. Stephen had made a great effort to keep his temper for her sake, even when, in desperation to get out of the traffic, he took a wrong turning and found himself on the old main road north instead of the motorway – even then he kept control of himself.

That night, in Tournus, he had gone to bed before Vi herself.

'I'm knackered,' he'd told her. She had turned to look at him across the dinner table as though surprised to see him there. Then she had smiled and her eyes had lit up again. She'd ordered a brandy for him. 'Take it upstairs. A night-cap.'

That was more like it.

She had enjoyed the market in the morning. The hotel was right on the central square, near the town hall. Stephen had got up early to move the van to a side-street. As they ate breakfast, they exchanged remarks in low voices about the men who came in and ordered drinks at the bar.

Vi was once again taking an interest in her surroundings: the bright colours of the liquid in the men's glasses, amber, green, and pink; the cocker spaniel that begged by the crossed legs of Madame. Madame had dressed up for market day. She wore a chunky bead necklace, the colour of cochineal; huge matching earrings that shook as she talked; and a navy-blue overall dress with buttons undone towards the hem so that a frill of pink lace showed above her pale stockinged knees. The men tossed back their heads and downed their drinks in one gulp. Madame crossed and recrossed her legs and laughed. Outside, the square filled with stalls. A red bus arrived and let down its sides to form long, staggered shelves of goods.

Vi was as intrigued by this as he himself. They discussed the possibilities of adapting such a vehicle for journeys. 'You'd have the shelves opening inwards rather than outwards,' he said. 'And you could put mattresses on the shelves,' she suggested. But where the shelves would go in the daytime defeated them.

Near the stall where they had chosen three kinds of cheese, there was a rail of dresses, each dress strangely bulging at the bosom. Vi peeped inside one of the dresses. 'Wire,' she had mouthed at him. 'Wire hangers shaped – shaped like that.' They both turned away from the approaching salesman to hide their amusement.

Vi was back to normal. In his head he began listening to Kiss playing 'Creatures of the Night' at full volume.

Archéodrome, announced a brown sign which portrayed a Viking-like character staring fiercely at the passing traffic.

In the Haute-Savoie, the brown signs beside the road had been more light-hearted. Small figures with large noses and big boots had marched up triangles to inform the passing motorists that this was an ideal area for climbing.

Dijon, la capitale des Ducs.

Aire du Bois des Corbeaux.

Véhicules lents.

Prix pique-nique.

Where would she and Steve eat their pique-nique today?

Vi put on her glasses to study the map. They had reached the page of the motoring book which showed Paris. Might they really reach the Channel tonight? An Annecy travel agent had recommended the Le Havre–Southampton crossing and given them a timetable. Her eye was caught by the name of a town just north of Paris: Beauvais. Le Havre was north-west of Paris.

Beauvais would not be too long a detour . . . She could find his grave.

The sight of a grave was proof of death. The Argentine mothers could not believe their missing children were dead. Without proof, mourning had no beginning, no end.

She realized that the low growling noise which Stephen had been making for a while was in fact singing. He missed his music. She had put her foot down firmly at the start of the journey; he was not to play cassettes. He had been very good about this. Should she let him play just one cassette now, when they were so near the end of their journey? No.

Instead of having a picnic, perhaps they could go into Paris and have a slap-up meal to celebrate? No. That would be tempting providence.

'If we reach Le Havre tonight, we must ring your parents,' she called to Steve over the noise of the engine.

'We'll get there easily. If nothing else goes wrong,' Steve shouted back.

Vi decided she would not mention Beauvais until they stopped for lunch. Depending on what point they had reached by then, she'd know if the detour was possible.

The rain had let up but the atmosphere was murky. They were passing a castle on a hill. Twelfth century, said the brown sign. It was a fairy-tale illustration of a castle and Vi could almost see the princess locked in the tower. In the curving fields below the castle, white dots were visible in swathes of mist.

'Charollais,' said Vi.

'Yes. Great for Rumpelstiltskin,' said Steve.

'No. The cows,' said Vi. Still, his education was not completely full of holes.

Besides, he knew things she didn't know. She searched her mind for examples: the makes of cars and motor-bikes, for a start. Then he knew how to open things. Many had been the occasion when he had rescued her from a battle with a carton of orange juice, a packet of biscuits, a portion of marmalade. He had fathomed the plumbing of several bathrooms for her, saving her from taps which wouldn't turn on and, worse, taps that wouldn't turn off. He had locked, and unlocked, unlockable doors. He had understood all the gadgets in the Annecy hotel and made them work, so that she could make instant coffee and watch television, turn the heating on at night, and telephone the reception if need be.

Without Steve – well, without Steve she would not be here at all.

A glow of wellbeing spread through her.

It was a wet, grey day. Her feet were cold in the canvas shoes she had foolishly put on in the sun of Tournus. She was being driven along in a ramshackle old van by a nineteen-year-old. It was noisy, draughty and uncomfortable. Yet she was happy. She was no longer looking forward to anything better, nor regretting anything past.

She had relinquished, in Annecy, the idea of Patrick that she had nursed since his death.

'What are paires?' asked Steve.

'*Poires*,' answered Vi. 'Why? Do you want to buy some?'

'No. That game.'

He was waving a ham roll in the direction of the building in front of them. They were parked in the forecourt of a motorway stop. The outskirts of Paris had taken them by surprise and there was no better place to eat their picnic.

Alimentation, Boissons, Change, Librairie, she read. *Jeu de la fortune, Faites les paires et devenez millionaire.*

'Oh, *paires,*' she said. '*Paires* are pairs.'

'I thought so,' said Steve smugly. 'Easy language, French, isn't it.'

Vi smiled. 'If it's that easy –'

'It just didn't make sense at school,' he replied at once. 'Nothing did. Total waste of time. Let's try and make a pair and become millionaires.'

Vi suddenly felt sickened. A jumble of words, phrases and half-formed images came to mind; a kind of instant collage of supermarkets, bingo, football pools, football hooligans, double your money, take-over bids, flotations, drugs, permissive society, Aids, the swinging Sixties, you've never had it so good, get rich quick, I'm all right Jack, butter mountains, wine lakes, boat people, famine victims, hypothermia, gas chambers, napalm, hijacks, high-rise, air-raid shelters, Chernobyl, Star Wars . . .

'A war to end all wars,' she said aloud. She noticed Steve's puzzlement. How she wished that somehow this young man beside her . . . 'Something's gone so very wrong. Yet so many people tried to make things so much better for everyone. To make things fair. Instead . . .' She paused. It was said that children were their parents' stake in the future. Steve, sitting beside her, was her stake in the future. She wished she could somehow mould him . . . 'Instead we're all urged to play the game and become millionaires.'

'What's wrong with that? Come on, let's buy a ticket. Someone's got to win. It could be us.'

She had no influence over Steve. He was not her child. Besides, it was absurd to think that simply by dissuading him from taking part in a lottery he would be influenced for ever against materialism.

North of Beauvais young men of his age had died defending their country.

She would take him there.

Their own bloody fault. Steve had said that a few days

ago. What had they been talking about then? Vietnam? 'Steve, as we want to get the ten-thirty ferry, we've got lots of time, haven't we?'

He nodded over a mouthful of bread and pâté.

'I was wondering if we could visit the cemetery at Beauvais . . . It's not far out of our way.' She handed him the map.

She became aware that his startlingly blue eyes were watching her and she looked away.

He had forgotten about the lottery but there was something else about the illuminated sign that sickened her. *Faites les paires et devenez millionaire.* One more image came to mind. She saw again the photograph of two laughing faces. Patrick and Ivy had been a pair and she had never known.

As they drove on, Vi returned once more to the roundabout of questions which she thought she had left behind in Annecy. Only a few hours ago she had felt calm and happy, certain that she had laid that ghost. But ghosts – delusions – carried around for nearly sixty years were not so easily laid.

I'm knackered, Steve had said last night. She had looked at his tired face across the table and been brought with a jolt into the present. By brooding on the past she was ignoring the needs of the person at her side. She had bought him a brandy and, after he had gone to bed, ordered one for herself.

Drinking it slowly in a corner of the bar, she had chided herself for her foolishness. She was in danger of repeating once again the mistake she had been making all her life.

She had deluded herself about Patrick. It was only after his death that she had created the fantasy that he had been the man in her life.

While he was alive she had thought no such thing.

Was this true? She searched her mind for recollections of the twenties. Had there been any moment, any glance, any hint, on either side? Perhaps there had been a moment . . .

Hadn't he once put an arm around her? Or had she only imagined that in later years? She could remember the occasional meeting. He had come to the house a couple of times. She had met him in London. He had taken her out to lunch. Yes, at the Trocadero. A celebration of some sort. She struggled with her elusive memory. He'd been asked to go to Germany for some reason. It must have been something to do with his journalism. Something to do with airships. Of course – it came to her suddenly. The first transatlantic flight of the Zeppelin. The ZR3. That was in 1924.

The photograph. It was the following year that she had gone up to London with the five-pound piece in her handbag. She had been twenty-five. Ivy had crossed the room and snapped the album shut. She should have understood *then* from the words on the brown paper backing. She had seen a shaving brush on the bathroom shelf. How could she have been so obtuse? The reason why Ivy had been disturbed to see her was that it was not a photographic model in the studio upstairs but Patrick.

Yet, remembering this occasion as the van slowly skirted Paris in Saturday afternoon traffic, Vi found it hard to work out how she could be so sure now; and how she could have been so unaware then.

Ivy and Patrick had obviously not wanted her to know.

Why had they not wanted her to know?

Could it be that they understood what she felt for Patrick?

But her feelings for Patrick had only been formulated in later years.

Perhaps she *had* been in love with Patrick. Perhaps she had been in love with him and not realized it. Ivy had realized it and, by leaving the photograph face-down on the top of the pile in the box, had at last let her know. Ivy was telling her that they had both loved Patrick.

'Vi! Vi! Map-read!'

Stephen was needing directions.

She seized the map guiltily and, putting on her glasses, found the right page.

'Take the autoroute E1 as far as the turning to Mantes, then a red road north, the 183 to Beauvais.'

The cemetery was on the outskirts of Beauvais, Vi learnt from the tourist information office. The girl behind the desk gave her a map of the town on which she had drawn arrows and a circled asterisk at the edge of the page.

'It's very close,' she told Steve as she returned to the van. She had expected the cemetery to be out in the countryside some distance north of the town.

It took them only five minutes to drive there. Steve parked just before the gates, on the opposite side of the road. He said he would wait in the van.

Vi did not attempt to persuade him otherwise although up to this moment she had hoped he would join her. She had imagined a green sward studded with thousands of crosses, a place whose strength of atmosphere could not fail to affect him. But the urban cemetery across the road, with high wrought-iron entrance gates and enclosed by walls and railings, appeared parochial in the extreme; the last resting place for the honest, hard-working citizens of Beauvais; a place that could only stir the hearts of those who lived in the town.

'I won't be long,' she said.

She waited at the pedestrian crossing for a pause in the stream of traffic heading north to Amiens. No car stopped to let her cross. Eventually there was a gap long enough. She hurried across as fast as she could, wishing she had brought her stick.

Perhaps the gates would be locked. Perhaps this was not the right cemetery at all. The girl in the tourist office might have misunderstood her.

The gates were not locked. Vi pulled back the heavy iron latch and walked in, closing the gate carefully behind her.

The roar of traffic faded as she followed the central path towards a flagpole. It had begun to rain again, gently, persistently. On either side of the path stretched rows of identical, pinkish-stone crosses set with metal plates. On each the same message was inscribed beneath the name: *Mort pour la France.*

Vi turned to walk between the rows. Every so often among the crosses there was a white stone. These, Vi saw, bore English names. *G.E. Nash, Royal Australian Air Force, 8th July 1944, aged 20. Our all. Flying Officer P.F. Sturgess, Navigator/Wireless Operator, Royal Air Force, 11th July 1944, aged 21.*

This was certainly a war cemetery but it was the wrong war. She walked on. *Mort pour la France. Mort pour la France.* She felt her eyes filling with tears at the repetition. *Lt E. Mc.D. Jarvis, Royal Air Force, 16th June 1918.* She read the date with a sudden bound of her heart. *At the going down of the sun and in the morning we will remember him.*

Then, in the next row, she found what she had been looking for: *Lt T.R. Sharpe, Royal Air Force, 16th June 1918.*

Tom, her heart cried. She read and reread the name. The stone was set, as were all the stones, in long flower beds planted with dwarf rose bushes, some of which were in flower. The shrub in front of Tom's stone bore no flowers and this hurt her. She should have brought flowers for his grave. She had been cutting a rose when she had learnt of his death.

She told herself that now, seeing his grave, she could believe in his death. She made herself think of his bones lying beneath the earth, so close to her. She kept repeating his name but now as though she were calling to him, questioning him.

At last she moved on, ready but unwilling to leave the cemetery. She could not stop reading the messages engraved on the stones.

Mort pour la France.
Mort pour la France.
To live in hearts we leave behind is not to die.

Steve shifted his position and opened his eyes. It was too

cold to sleep. He wished he hadn't left Greece. Where were they now? He must have dozed off because he found it hard to work out what he was doing by himself in the van, parked in a busy main road in some town or other. It was raining. Traffic whooshed past the van constantly. He wiped the windscreen with the palm of his hand to see out more clearly.

A short distance ahead was a pedestrian crossing. On the near side of the road there was a woman waiting with a pram. She was waving urgently to someone on the far side. An oncoming lorry flashed its headlights. Steve saw an old lady hesitating a few yards onto the crossing from the other side of the road. The lorry blared its horn. The old lady turned and regained the pavement as the lorry swept past. Vi!

Steve leapt out of the van, darted across the road at the first opportunity and reached Vi before she made another attempt. He took her elbow firmly and steered her across the road, holding his free arm high in the air to stop the traffic.

'Buggers, aren't they,' he said.

'I must change my shoes. They're sopping wet.'

He found the shoes she wanted, wrapped in newspaper at the bottom of her suitcase.

'Can you see a little green towel too, Steve? Near the top, I think.'

She rubbed her stockinged feet dry with difficulty. Steve climbed into the front of the van and helped her get her shoes on.

'Thank you, dear,' she said.

'Did you find it?' he asked.

'Yes,' she said. 'I wonder – have we time for a cup of tea?'

'Plenty of time.' He returned to the back of the van to brew up.

'I'll stay in the front. You can pass it to me when it's ready.'

As he waited for the kettle to boil, he was aware of Vi's silence and stillness. He tried to imagine what it was like, seeing the grave of someone you had loved, someone who had been killed so many years ago.

'Do you think you'd better change into something dry?' he suggested when he handed her the mug of tea. 'I'll find something in your suitcase.'

'Oh no, I won't bother. I'll soon dry off. This is all I need.' She clasped the mug with both hands. 'Come and sit in front.'

Perhaps she wanted to talk about Patrick, he thought. Settling himself in the driving seat, he asked, 'Are they all buried here?'

'All?' She looked puzzled. 'Oh, no, the main graveyards are in Flanders. Beauvais wasn't near the lines.'

'The lines, what lines?'

'The front. There was an airfield near here, used in both wars. There are airmen buried here from both wars.'

Steve struggled to make sense of this answer. 'But it didn't happen in wartime,' he said at last. 'I thought it crashed in 1930.'

Vi lowered her mug of tea and turned to look at him in wonder. 'Oh heavens. You thought I'd come to visit . . .'

'The R101 crashed at Beauvais.'

'Yes. So it did. You're right. But they weren't buried here. They were taken back to England. That was not why I wanted to come here. No, what Beauvais has always meant to me was the place where Tom was killed. My brother. I've wanted to visit Beauvais ever since but never quite managed it. Till now.'

They finished their tea in silence, absorbed with their own thoughts.

As they drove into the centre of town again to find the road to Rouen, they saw the cathedral looming ahead. It looked like a craggy hunk of rock split away from a mountain that had disappeared. There was something impressive but unfulfilled about its massive shape concentrated into such a small area. It bore aloft a diminutive turret. So much for so little. The phrase came into Vi's mind but she was not sure if she was thinking of the cathedral or the cemetery.

'Signs, Vi. Look out for signs.'

'Sorry,' she said. She should be helping Steve find the way.

Soon they were out in open countryside. The clouds had lifted and fitful sun lit beechwoods with a copper light. They drove through villages where deep-roofed houses lined the road, their windows shuttered against the traffic. There were half-timbered cottages with neat rows of vegetables growing in their gardens. Sheep grazed in orchards. Moving slowly across green fields were cows so fat they seemed to be filling their brown and white coats to bursting point; as though they were trying on the spotted coats of some much smaller animal, a seal for instance.

'Reminds me of Somerset,' said Vi.

'Never been there,' said Steve. They began a conversation about places they would like to visit but the strain of talking above the sound of the engine was too great. After Steve shouted, 'Let's drive on up to Scotland!' – a suggestion which made Vi laugh, they lapsed once more into silence.

So Vi had been visiting the grave of her brother Tom, thought Steve. He had been so convinced that Patrick was the reason for the Beauvais visit, he had not even bothered to ask her why she wanted to go there.

She had been totally dumbfounded by his misunderstanding. So maybe Patrick had not been Vi's man at all. He himself had created a romance for her that didn't exist.

Why, he wondered, had he been so keen to invent an Uncle Vi? It wasn't as though he was like his sisters, longing to see a Mills & Boon story in every chance meeting. He longed for a girlfriend but that didn't mean he thought everyone had to be part of a couple. He wasn't ever going to get married himself. Vi had had a perfectly reasonable life on her own. She seemed to him to be content. Perhaps he'd created a man not for her sake but for the man's. She'd been great on the journey; a restful person to be with.

It came to him that the reason for this was that she had not expected anything of him or from him.

He suddenly wanted to do something for her. Why not take her on up to Scotland? He'd said this as a joke, but why not really do it? Obviously they'd call in at home first. They'd be there in time for Sunday lunch. They could stay the night and then start off on Monday. He began planning the route.

Scotland! thought Vi. What a ridiculous idea – and how touching. To think that Steve should suggest continuing the trip . . .

You must get on very well, someone had said on the journey.

They did.

Was it because –

She turned aside from this for the moment. She remembered Stephen's intensely questioning, yet at the same time knowing, expression when she had asked if they could visit Beauvais. She now understood why he had looked at her like that. He had assumed it was because of Patrick that she wanted to go there. No wonder he had been so surprised to learn it was Tom's grave she had visited.

Even Steve thought she was in love with Patrick.

How complicated it all was, but she must persevere. She felt her whole life had been a muddle. If she could only work out what had happened . . .

She had loved Tom too much. Her love for him had not died with his death. It had prevented her from loving anyone else.

Patrick was Tom's friend. Perhaps, if Tom had lived, she could have loved Patrick. Instead he had turned to Ivy.

She remembered buying Steve a brandy. She had not noticed how tired he was, so busy had she been with her thoughts of the past. She'd seen this as a repetition on a minor scale of the mistake she had been making all her life. If in the 1920s she could have forgotten Tom, then she would have realized that she and Patrick might have loved each other. A scene in the summerhouse came to mind. Patrick had put an arm around her as she cried.

But maybe nothing was a mistake. Maybe we only act as we are bound to act. Her life had suited her. She had wanted nothing more.

And why was she so happy in Steve's company? Was it because it was a completely safe relationship? Safe, like that of brother and sister. Safe, because he was not a soldier and would not be buried at Beauvais.

They arrived in Le Havre in time to reserve tickets on the ten-thirty ferry, telephone home and have a meal before boarding.

The restaurant they chose, in a street of restaurants, was little more than a passageway in which the tables were crammed so close a party atmosphere was created. Steve and Vi found themselves in conversation with their neighbours. On one side was a French couple who lived in Le Havre. Vi dealt with the talking, translating every so often questions addressed to Steve. Steve meanwhile exchanged anecdotes and information with the English couple on the other side. Bottles of wine mounted up on the table. Glasses were raised, toasts were proposed, invitations issued, addresses exchanged.

'And next time you're in England,' Vi told her Le Havre friends, 'you must come and visit us.'

'Oh dear, I think I drank rather too much wine,' she said as they emerged from the restaurant.

They had left the van near the docks, a short walk away. The night air was chill after the warmth of the restaurant. Visit us, echoed in her mind. Yet she was returning to her empty cottage; while Steve was returning to his family.

The road crossed a waterway in which boats were moored. The sight brought home to them the fact that they had reached the Channel. They paused at the edge of a jetty and looked down. Dinghies, yachts, rowing boats and motor launches idled side by side, their mooring ropes dipping into the black water.

Steve thought: that is the sea. Those are boats. But there's something wrong and sad about it. He looked up at the sky and saw the half-moon shining brightly in scudding clouds which looked bruised by the moonlight. He thought: and that's the sky and that's the moon. But it's not the Greek moon and it's not the Greek sky. That is not the Greek sea and those are not Greek boats.

'I may be a bit drunk too,' he said to Vi. 'I'm wishing I'd never come home.'

Vi felt momentarily hurt. 'But I'm so glad you did. I wouldn't have missed the journey for the world.'

Steve turned to her quickly. 'Oh I didn't mean that,' he said. 'I just meant – I'll miss Greece.' He pulled his headband down over his nose, ran his fingers through his hair and pushed the band back into place. 'I'm glad about the journey too,' he said and then turned away. 'Come on. It's not over yet. We mustn't miss the boat.'

Stephen looked around the dining-room where only a month before he and Vi had eaten Sunday lunch.

He could see his father carving the roast pork at one end of the table, his mother serving vegetables at the other. He and Vi had exchanged looks across the table. His parents' interest in the journey had not lasted as long as the travellers' need to tell the tale. They had smiled at each other as his parents began to question him about his plans.

Vi had answered for him. 'We're thinking of continuing the journey up to Scotland.'

There had been consternation at this. 'As a doctor,' his father had said, 'I must insist that –'

'At *her* age!' someone was saying now.

The chairs were pushed back against the wall and the table was set with plates of sandwiches, sausage rolls, and various quiches.

'Steve!' His mother was beside him. 'Don't just stand there. Hand something round.'

He caught snatches of conversation.

'Do you know, she even wanted to go on up to Scotland! Can you imagine?'

'William's doing A-levels. It's Jonathan at Manchester.'

'Of course Diana lives in Scotland. Is she here?'

'On the kitchen floor.'

'Her daily found her.'

'No, we came by overnight train.'

'Knocked her head against the table, I thought.'

'No, heart.'

'She'd caught cold on the journey.'

'Or help Dad hand the sherry round.' That was his mother again.

'Who are all these people?' he asked her.

'Oh, Stephen,' said his mother crossly, 'you know them perfectly well. Just help. And for heaven's sake mingle. There's William over there. Go and talk to him.' She moved away, uttering little cries of hospitality. 'Do help yourselves! Have you a drink? Sherry, wine, whisky? Oh, Edith! How lovely to see you. How are you?'

Stephen helped himself to a sausage roll and looked across the room at his cousin William who had come all the way from Scotland with Aunt Diana. What on earth for? It seemed pointless to him. Vi had meant nothing to them.

He hadn't seen his cousins, William and Jonathan, for years. The last time had been a camping holiday in the Yorkshire Dales. The two families had met up. William and Jonathan had been Boy Scouts. They were insufferably scornful of the Winfields' tent, knots, and camp fires. Steve had called them Bill and John and they had had a fight, two against one. Steve did not want to cross the room and talk to William.

Oh, Vi, he thought.

'Steve! Take this round.' His father handed him a decanter of sherry. 'There's the vicar in that corner with Creedy. They need refills. Where's Vicky? We need more glasses.'

The level of noise in the room was mounting. It was a party atmosphere. It reminded him of the last meal in Le Havre.

On the ferry he and Vi had had a conversation about death.

He'd managed to get her a cabin after the boat sailed. He'd queued at the purser's office. But she hadn't been able to sleep. They'd taken blankets from the cabin and gone up on deck.

They'd leant over the rail, mesmerized by the bow waves creaming in the moonlight.

Vi had begun talking in a quiet hesitant way. 'I was just thinking of the Romans crossing the Channel. They were at the very edge of time as we are now. Hard to imagine, isn't it, someone in the past not knowing the future which for us is the past. Like the black sea. Time – no, life – lifetimes are like the sea. Each generation a wave breaking on the shore, a continual assault, a fresh discovery of the unknown, untouched future. And each life is like a particle of that wave that forms and peaks and breaks and reaches and touches the shore. You see, what I am thinking, Steve, is what you often say, "What's the point?" And it seems to me now at this moment that perhaps I've understood something. But as soon as you try and put it into words, it goes away . . .'

'So – try. What are you thinking?' he asked.

'The point is that there would be no point without life. Life itself is the point. Which as soon as you say it sounds absurd. I haven't wasted my life because it is enough simply to live. I'm thinking of the waves, the generations. The wave breaks, retreats, becomes part of the sea again, another wave breaks. It's a new wave but it's impossible to say in what way it is new or different from the one before or the one after. And as some waves have more effect – in storms they are bigger and more devastating, destructive – and sometimes constructive, creative, making inlets, shaping rocks – so there are waves of human history that have more effect and are remembered.

'Each wave is only a wave because of its individual molecules. Without those minute particles, there would be no wave. Without each human life there would be no human life.

'And the wave becomes part of the sea again, reforms – not the same wave but a similar wave – it dies and is born.

'We as individuals are not important but at the same time every individual is essential. When I am alive, I am visible as the wave is visible. When I die, I am not visible, but I still exist, part of the sea . . .'

Stephen, recalling this conversation as he watched the people who had gathered because of Vi's death, could hear her voice. He could remember the essence of what she had said but not the words themselves. He suddenly wanted very much to talk to her.

She had not said goodbye to him.

He had gone over once since their homecoming. She had left her canvas shoes in the van and these he had returned one afternoon. She gave him a cup of tea.

'There. Now I've made tea for *you*. Remember that awful camomile?'

She had a wood fire burning in her sitting-room. On a table by the window was a cardboard box filled with papers. More boxes were stacked in a corner of the room.

'I'm sorting things out a bit,' she said. 'I haven't much money except for this cottage which now, apparently, is worth an amazing sum. I'm thinking of selling up. I could spend the rest of my days travelling . . . I would like that trip to Scotland. Perhaps in the spring?'

In the spring, he agreed, they'd get in the van again.

'By then, of course, you'll have found a girl. You won't want to go travelling with an old woman like me.'

As he left, she handed him her father's binoculars. 'I'd like you to have these,' she said.

'But you'll want them,' he said.

'No, take them now . . .'

The binocular now hung from a hook in the hall.

He looked around the room. His mother and his aunt were facing each other, their heads thrown back, laughing. The vicar and Creedy, the solicitor, were deep in conversation. 'One up and one to go, then straight into the bunker,' said Creedy. Vi's neighbour and his sister Claire were talking about hairdressers. There was a group of three women, one of whom he thought he recognized. 'If you could manage the same hours for me as you did for Miss Sharpe . . .'

Vi was not here. Even in the church and at the grave beside the stones engraved with family names, she had been distant.

At the door into the hall he met his mother.

'Ah, Steve! Clean glasses in the kitchen. Will you bring them in?'

With the binoculars slung over his shoulder, he opened the front door.

'Steve! Where are you going? You are not going out, are you? Steve!'

He shut the front door behind him.

The motor-bike he had been assembling from spare parts was just about roadworthy, although it still needed a few bits to make it legal. But he did not want to go by bike. He wanted to take the van.

He was not yet sure where he would go. He drove out of the gates and past the house where his grandmother, Vi's sister, had lived. In the next road he passed the strangely shaped house which he now knew had been called the Lodge. Vi had lived there and, before her, someone called Sam who had been the gardener of the big house. The road beside the Lodge must have been the drive. He thought he might turn down it but decided not to. It was silly to look for something that no longer existed. Perhaps he would visit Vi's cottage. He took the road that led down into the town but, before he reached the traffic lights at the foot of the hill, he had another idea. He thought of the place where they had picnicked, the high round hill that had been so good for flying kites.

He tried to remember where in the surrounding countryside this hill was. He had only gone there as a child, a passenger. Turning in a side-road, all he was certain of was that it lay in the opposite direction, in an area which he had had no reason to visit for years. He drove up the hill again, past the Lodge, past the turning to his home, and on past all the new estates until he reached the sports centre. He could remember this being built. The narrow, country crossroads that had once marked this spot had vanished beneath the new dual carriageway.

For several minutes he drove up and down side-roads, thinking as he did so how stupid he was being. He could not ask the way. He could hear the absurd question. 'Where's the crossroads that used to be here? And does the road that went straight over lead to a high round hill?'

Then he found himself approaching a flyover which crossed the dual carriageway. It seemed to him he was heading in the right direction. After a while the urban development gave way to fields and woods. Whenever there was a fork in the road, he let his instinct lead him one way or the other. He grew more and more certain that he was approaching the right area. He recognized the name of a village along the way.

The road dipped into a wooded valley. Yes, this was right. Soon there would be a track to the left which, if it was not too muddy, cars had been able to drive along. After another mile, the track appeared. Steve turned into it.

A short distance along the track a gate barred the way. Before the gate there was a wide parking area, a National Trust sign and a notice urging visitors to take their litter home.

Steve was glad to see that he was the only visitor. He parked the van and got out. Then he leant across the driver's seat for his binoculars. As he did so, he noticed something small and silver wedged at the back of the seat. It was a hundred-lira coin. Vi had wanted him to hand it in at the travel office. 'Someone will be missing it,' she'd said. Even if she had realized that a hundred lira was virtually worthless, she would have wanted to return it to its owner. He smiled. Already he felt her closer.

With the binoculars slung round his neck, he climbed over the gate. The track led up through a wood. Vi would be telling him what birds they might see in the wood. He himself could see no birds at all but then something gave a screech. 'A jay,' he heard in his mind. Well, he might be right.

'Wait for me, wait for me.' He could see his sisters running on ahead. They had reached the part where the track emerged from the woods. His mother and father and Aunty Vi were nowhere to be seen. No doubt he was ahead of them.

He turned and saw a couple of walkers with a dog at the edge of the track. They had come out of the wood and he saw, with relief, that they were heading for the gate.

He walked on. Soon he had reached the end of the track and the lower slopes of the high round hill. It was just as steep a climb as he remembered and by the time he reached the top he was hot and panting.

'Fresh air and exercise, that's what you need.'

The view stretched away to the south in receding bands of russet, sage green and blue, framed by tall trees which grew halfway down the far slope.

'Scots pines.'

There had been Scots pines in the Annecy park.

His kite had been blue with a red and yellow tail. It had risen high into the air, higher than the kites of Vicky and Claire. He had run down the hill with the kite dancing above him, the cleat of string held fast in his fist. Then he had tripped and fallen. The wind whipped the kite away and abandoned it at the very top of the nearest pine. No one heard his cries. He eventually trudged back up the hill to find Aunty Vi sitting on the tartan rug.

'Oh, Aunty Vi,' he cried, burying his face in her lap.

Stephen glanced behind him as though there on the hill he would see the tartan rug and Aunty Vi and the picnic basket.

'Oh, Vi,' he cried, clenching his fists. He looked up at the sky as though he might see her face. It had been a wet day but now the clouds were breaking up, blown by a brisk east wind. He turned away from the wind and saw the sun had emerged from cloud. It hung low over the horizon, sending shafts of golden light towards the hill. He knew that tears were streaming down his face. 'I can't help it,' he told himself. 'It's too much, it's too beautiful. I miss her.'

'Oh Steve, don't be such a sausage.' She had pulled his socks up and told him there was more than one kite in the world. 'You just liked that one because it belonged to you. Well, we can find another one and that will belong to you in just the same way.'

'Yes but –' began Steve. He held the binoculars in his hands. 'But I'll miss *you*.'

Then she spoke again and this time he was certain that it was not a voice from the past nor a voice that he imagined. It was Vi, speaking clearly to him, giving him a message that he would remember.

'To live in hearts we leave behind is not to die,' she told him.